WHALE HARBOR SISTERS

SALTWATER SUNSETS BOOK TWO

FIONA BAKER

JOIN MY NEWSLETTER

If you love beachy, feel-good women's fiction, sign up to receive my newsletter, where you'll get free books, exclusive bonus content, and info on my new releases and sales!

CHAPTER ONE

"What do you think, Peaches?" Marty Sims murmured, placing a decorative pumpkin first one way and then another in the window box display.

Her orange cat, Peaches, looked up at her inquiringly, her eyes huge and adorable. Marty smiled down at her, cooing at her for a moment and setting aside the pumpkin for the time being so that she could scoop Peaches up and scratch between her ears. Peaches began purring, vibrating gently in Marty's arms as Marty snuggled her.

"You're the best work associate ever, do you realize that?" she cooed. "So sweet, aren't you?"

Peaches purred even harder, if that was possible. Marty petted her a few more times and then set her down, picking up the pumpkin again and finally settling on placing it jauntily on a decorative chair in the window display. Next, she picked up a wreath decorated with orange, red, and yellow leaves and played around with it, trying it first in one spot, then another.

She was putting up a few fall decorations in her nautical interior design shop, Sand 'n' Things. Her shop was mostly beach themed, but she figured she should add in a few fall decorations for some festive autumn flair. It clashed a bit with her meticulously curated beach themed items, but she knew what would sell, and it was fall, so fall decorations needed to make an appearance in her shop, like it or not. Peaches rubbed against her legs, winding between them in figure eights while Marty arranged a cute wooden sign that said "Hello Fall!" next to the wreath.

Slipping outside, Marty looked at the window display from the sidewalk, studying it carefully and then giving a firm nod. She was pleased with the way it had turned out and she knew that it would lure many shoppers into her store.

Stepping back into her shop, she locked the front door behind her and flipped the sign around so that it read "Closed." It was past seven in the evening and she knew she should really go home—it wasn't like the work she was doing couldn't wait until tomorrow —but it wasn't like she had anyone to go home to.

Well, she amended in her mind, *not any humans, that is.*

Marty looked around her shop, checking to see that all was in order. As always, everything was neat as a pin, the way she liked to keep it. Darla called her obsessive, but Marty couldn't help it. She liked things to be just so. It made her feel safe, and what was so wrong with that? She wandered over to a display and adjusted a picture frame a fraction of an inch, nodding in satisfaction with how it made the display look more polished.

Pausing, she looked around at her little shop, satisfaction filling her as she took in the fruits of her labors. Her satisfaction, however, was mingled with a certain sense of melancholy.

She loved her shop—it was her dream, and she had worked very hard to make it as successful as it was—but there was something sad about not having anyone to share her success with.

Well, no one besides Peaches, and Peaches didn't really count.

Not for the first time, she wondered if quietly minding her little interior design shop was going to be her only lot in life. She appreciated stability, perhaps more than anyone else she knew, but she was also lonely.

I'd like to be married, she admitted to herself silently.

Yes, Marty would love to be married, but so far no one had ever really fit the bill. Her mouth turned down as she considered the various failed one-time dates she had gone on. Most men wanted women who were more adventurous and exciting than she was, or at least that was what she thought privately.

Maybe if I was more fun-loving, I would have already found a husband.

The thought made her stomach clench, and she hurried to her office to power down her computer and finish locking up the shop, not wanting to dwell on that disconcerting thought. It only made her feel worse about herself, and she already *did* feel bad about the fact that she wasn't more adventurous like other people she knew. She knew she had many wonderful qualities, knew that there was plenty that was good about herself and her personality, but she felt like those all got overshadowed by the fact that she was so cautious and risk-averse.

"Come on, Peaches," Marty called. "Let's go home."

Peaches trotted to the back of the shop and waited for Marty to scoop her up. Marty bent down and gathered her cat into her arms, dropping her into her large tote bag and then left through the back of her shop, locking the door behind her. Outside, the sun had already set but the sky was still streaked in pinks and oranges. Marty took a moment to appreciate the beauty of the twilight sky and then climbed into her car.

The drive back to her house wasn't too long, so Marty spent it in silence, simply thinking. As she drove, her thoughts turned back to her desire to get married. Her woeful dating history went back to high school, even. Boys hadn't really been interested in her then, either. In fact, she had only ever had one real crush—Wyatt Jameson.

Wyatt, with his sandy brown hair and gray eyes had taken her heart by storm. She had sat beside him in her freshman algebra class and he'd turned to her with his crooked smile, asking if she wanted to study together, and her heart had been lost.

The crazy thing about it was that he totally shouldn't have been her type. After all, he was cool and adventurous and athletic. He rode ATVs for fun, something she would never dream of doing—far too risky. But for Wyatt, she had thought about it sometimes. She had liked him for so long, but it had never come to anything.

After high school, he had left Whale Harbor to go work with his dad in Yarmouth, where his dad ran a quad and dirt bike restoration shop. She still saw him from time to time whenever he swung into town to visit his mom. He would call her up out of the blue to see her, always at the last minute and spur of the moment, but Marty would cling to those unexpected visits.

Of course, she never knew when she would hear from him after each visit. He would go back to Yarmouth and she wouldn't hear from him for weeks, sometimes even months. After a while, she had finally begun to steel her heart against him. He had just been too inconsistent, and life had gotten in the way and he had come to Whale Harbor less and less.

It's probably for the best that it didn't work out, she thought sadly, parking her car in her driveway and grabbing her tote bag, Peaches in tow. *I shouldn't keep dwelling on the past like this.*

She had just unlocked her front door and let Peaches out of the tote bag when she felt her phone buzzing in her pocket. She fished it out to see that her sister, Darla Sims, was calling. She quickly answered the phone.

"Hey, sis, what's up?"

"Nothing much. Just calling to say hi."

Marty smiled. Now that her sister had moved back to Whale Harbor permanently, they had become closer than ever.

"Well, hi! How are you? How's Rick doing?"

Marty could practically hear Darla smiling through the phone.

"Rick is good, and so am I. He surprised me with roses last night, for no reason at all!"

"Aww, that's so sweet. I bet you loved that."

"I really did," Darla said with a happy sigh. "I still have to pinch myself sometimes. I can't believe that our relationship is real, or that *the* Rick Maroney loves me."

"Of course he loves you!"

"I'm just some art nerd. He was a jock in high school!"

Marty grinned. "Come on, you've got to let that go. We're not in high school any more."

"No, we're not," Darla agreed. "Speaking of people from high school, guess who just moved back to town?"

"Who?"

"Wyatt Jameson."

Marty felt her mouth drop open. "You're kidding," she breathed, taken aback.

She had just been thinking about Wyatt and now, as if summoned by her thoughts, he was not only being talked about but he had moved back to Whale Harbor? Marty couldn't wrap her mind around it.

"Nope, not kidding."

Marty gulped. "Do you have any more details?"

"Why?" Darla asked, a slyly laughing note in her voice. "Is somebody interested?"

Marty could feel herself flushing. "No! Besides, he's married, isn't he?"

"Actually, he and his wife split up. He's single again, and word on the street is that he's here to stay."

Marty realized that she was holding the phone so tightly her knuckles were turning white and she consciously forced herself to relax her grip. Her heart was thudding in her chest, even as she tried to take deep, calming breaths. She didn't want to feel this way, didn't want to have a reaction to the news that Wyatt had come back to Whale Harbor. It had nothing to do with her—the days of Marty and Wyatt had long since passed, and she would do well to remember that.

She searched her mind desperately for a change of subject. "So, how is your art going?" she blurted out.

Thankfully, Darla took the bait and let the subject of Wyatt drop.

"Actually, Rick and I have been painting together a lot more lately. We even had a contest the other day."

"Oh?"

"Mmhmm. We were painting outside and we were both painting the sunset, so it just kind of evolved into a competition."

"So, who won?"

Darla laughed. "I'm honestly not sure. We ended up just sharing tips and tricks while we worked and I think we forgot all about winning."

"Some contest," Marty teased. "You know what's crazy? You came to Whale Harbor from New York, one of the art capitals of the world, and it seems that you're more inspired here than you ever were there."

"Well, maybe it's because I found love here," Darla said softly.

Marty became serious, then too. "That may very well be a huge part of it. I'm happy for you, sis."

"Thanks. Hey, let's get together for dinner soon."

"Deal."

Marty ended the call and slid her phone back into her pocket, finally closing the front door behind her and leaning against it. She blew out a deep breath, feeling tears prickling at the corners of her eyes. She was happy for her sister, so happy. But... sometimes it hurt, too, watching her sister have something that she herself may never have.

Sighing, Marty picked up her tote and hung it up in its spot in the coat closet, carefully placing it so that it didn't disturb her coats, which were perfectly lined up in order of color. The rest of her house was similarly meticulous. It was well-decorated with a nautical theme, and each and every piece had been carefully curated and placed with intention. Even with a cat in the house, not a thing was out of place. Marty breathed in the soothing calm of her home, trying to let go of the sadness that simmered just below the surface. Darla's words about how inspiring love had been for her came back to mind, and Marty tried to shove them away.

As she did every night, Marty went into the kitchen and brewed a cup of tea to drink while she read a book. She had the same ritual every night and she found it comforting but, just as she had felt at the shop, it also felt a little bit empty. Her life was perfect on the outside, but she knew, deep down, that something was missing.

The real question lay before her, glaring and obvious. Was she brave enough to seek out the missing piece in her life?

CHAPTER TWO

Wyatt Jameson walked briskly down the sidewalk toward the Clown Fish Eatery, his stomach grumbling as he went. Ever since he had moved back to Whale Harbor, he'd been meaning to make it over to his favorite diner, and today he finally had the time. He rubbed his hands together, already dreaming about the crab scramble with rye toast on the side.

He'd pretty much been living on fast food and ramen since he'd moved back, so busy cleaning up the property he'd purchased for his quad/biking shop that he'd had practically no time to go grocery shopping or sit down for a decent meal. Still, despite how hectic his schedule had been, he couldn't be more happy with how Wyatt's Quads was coming together.

Pushing open the door to Clown Fish Eatery, Wyatt breathed in the delicious aromas of good food and stepped inside.

Rose Smith, the grandmotherly owner of the eatery, bustled up to him, her faded blue eyes twinkling as she threw her arms around him. Rose was a plump woman of indeterminate age. Wyatt would have guessed she was in her early seventies, although he couldn't recall a time when she hadn't looked exactly as she did now. She was spry and light on her feet despite her plumpness, and she wore her fluffy white hair in a bun at the back of her head, often with a pencil or pen stuck through it.

"As I live and breathe," she said, stepping back to look at him. "It's Wyatt Jameson!"

"In the flesh, ma'am," he said, grinning down at her.

Rose surveyed him critically. "And a bit of a mess, too!" she remarked, pointing to the grease stain on his shirt and the dirt on his forearm. Wyatt looked down at himself, noting that he had missed a few spots when washing up to come to the diner.

"Hazards of the job," he remarked lightly.

"And what job has you this busy on a Saturday

morning?" she demanded, hands on her hips. "I'm sure you work too hard, son. It's the weekend after all!"

"I'm setting up a quad and biking shop here in Whale Harbor," Wyatt told her. "And there's just so much to do to get everything ready. It'll be worth it in the end, though. I'm excited to be offering a closer option for people who go to the dunes in Cape Cod."

Rose nodded understandingly. "There are always competitions going on over there. Those dunes have such a hold on people—especially the young people!"

"They do," Wyatt agreed. "The dunes are a lot of fun! All adventurous souls, regardless of age, love them. And it's not just competitive riding that goes on there, there's plenty of recreational riding. I'm sure my shop will stay plenty busy."

"I'm sure it will, young man," Rose said, patting his hand kindly.

Without thinking, Wyatt looked above Rose's head and did a quick scan of the eatery, looking on instinct for Marty. He knew that, even though she no longer worked there full time since her business had taken off, she still worked the Saturday shift out of loyalty. Rose cocked her head to the side, seeming to notice his distraction.

"Are you looking for someone?"

"Is Marty here? I was hoping to catch up with her," he replied, still looking around.

Marty was one of his dearest friends, and he had always made it a point to visit her when he would come back from helping his dad in Yarmouth. Those visits had stopped over the years, but he had always wondered how she was doing and if she was happy. Marty, with her kind, quiet ways, had always been an anchor in his erratic life, and he had a very tender place in his heart for their friendship.

"She's actually not here today," Rose was replying, pulling Wyatt's attention back to the present. "I gave her the day off, and she needed it! She works so hard and I told her she deserved to have a full weekend for once."

"That was kind of you."

Rose flapped her hands at that. "Oh, pshaw! I can't remember the last time Marty *didn't* work a Saturday here. She's so steady and dependable, you know, and fiercely loyal to the diner, but I insisted she take today off. She needs a break, poor thing! She works so hard."

"I'm sure she does," Wyatt agreed. "Marty is a gem."

"Steady as they come, that one."

"Sounds like Marty," Wyatt agreed, smiling softly. Marty always had been steady, nothing like him and his spontaneous ways. It was something he had always admired about her.

"Now then," Rose said, twinkling her blue eyes at him, "you look like you could use a good meal! You're much too thin. Haven't you been eating?"

"Yes, but not good food like you serve here," he teased.

"Well, I'm glad you came in, then," she said briskly. "We can fix that right away!"

"That's why I came in," Wyatt told her cheerfully. "How about I sit at that table with a view of the bay?"

"Perfect. Becky will be over to take your order in a jiffy and you just eat up, young man. I expect to see a fully clean plate when you're through!"

Wyatt saluted her and grinned. "I think I can handle that."

Rose led him over to the table he had indicated and poured him a cup of coffee before bustling off to tend to other customers. Wyatt relaxed in his seat, looking out at the boats bobbing in the bay. From here they looked small, but he knew many of them were rather large. The sight filled him with a calm satisfaction, the way all the sights of Whale Harbor did. It was good to finally be back home and, after the tumult of his divorce, it was exactly what his ravaged soul needed.

Just then Becky, a gawky red-headed teenage waitress, came up to him. She pushed her sliding glasses up to the top of her nose again, where they immediately slid back down. "Good morning. What can I get for you?"

Wyatt didn't even need the menu that sat in front of him. "I'll have the crab scramble with rye toast on the side, please."

Becky scribbled down his order. "Coming right up," she said, scooping up his menu. "Do you need more coffee?"

Wyatt shook his head. "I'm good for now, thanks."

Becky nodded, pushing her glasses up again, and then hurried off to place his order in the kitchen. Wyatt took a sip of his coffee, wincing a little as it burned his tongue. He should've blown on it first, but he'd acted without thinking, the way he often did.

The little incident reminded him of Marty again. She would have stirred her coffee, waiting patiently for it to cool enough to take a cautious sip. The thought made him smile to himself. Oh, but he missed her and her soothing presence in his life. Resting his elbows on the table, Wyatt looked out at the bay again and considered whether he should go visit her over at Sand 'n' Things. He would love to see her again and catch up, but he wasn't sure if he should.

There was no real reason not to, just his dratted nerves. Wyatt had always been a confident person, but his divorce had made him more wary and nervous, especially as he rediscovered who he was as a single man, instead of a married man. He really wanted to reconnect with his old friend, but... but what if things were different now, what if the connection they had always shared was no longer there?

Wyatt chewed the inside of his lip, second-guessing himself. He just wasn't sure if it was a good idea or not.

Just then, Becky returned with his crab scramble and rye toast, setting it down in front of him. Wyatt thanked her, holding back a smile as she tripped over her own feet while walking away. He remembered the days of being a gangly teenager and feeling like his hands and feet were too big for his body. Picking up his fork, he took a bite of the crab scramble and only just held back a groan of pleasure.

Wow, real food just tastes so good, he thought, taking another bite.

This was a far sight better than a squashed hamburger from a seedy fast food joint or a packet of cheap ramen. Eagerly, Wyatt took a bite of his rye toast, munching happily. Even though the food was delicious, he found his thoughts wandering back to Marty as he ate. In his hectic and erratic life, she had been a constant for him, an anchor of sorts, and he truly missed her.

She had been the only person he had always made it a point to visit when he would make trips back to Whale Harbor, and he really *did* want to see her again.

His memories of her were wrapped up in a glow of soft contentment, something that had been very much missing in his life since he and Helen had gotten divorced. Well, really, long before that. Things with his ex-wife had been bad for a long time before they finally pulled the trigger and filed for divorce.

So now, ravaged as he was by everything that had happened, Wyatt longed for the comfort of a good chat with his oldest friend, Marty. The question was whether he would be able to get over his strange case of nerves and actually make it happen.

CHAPTER THREE

"Oh, you poor babies," Marty breathed, crouching down to look under the latticework of her front porch. "You must be starving!"

The two stray kittens underneath her porch mewed back pitifully, all high-pitched and pathetic. Marty's heart squeezed at the sound and she stretched her hand toward them, simply holding it there and waiting for them to approach and sniff it. The more curious of the two trotted forward, sniffing at her hand delicately and then, after a moment, rubbing against her hand, hoping for pets. Marty complied, delighted. Made braver by its sibling's success, the other kitten came forward and sniffed at her too.

When they were well acquainted, Marty

reached out and picked up the two kittens, barely bigger than the palm of her hand. They were so tiny, so thin, that it made her heart ache.

"Come on, we'd better get you inside and get you fed," she murmured, cuddling them close.

Inside the house, her cat Peaches meowed loudly, wondering about the new occupants of the house. The two stray kittens trembled in her hands.

"Be nice," Marty ordered. "We have guests."

Gently, she laid them down in a cardboard box with a towel laid at the bottom for padding, then hurried to make them a bowl of soft cat food with a little bit of milk on the side. She brought it over to them and they attacked it, lapping at the milk and gobbling down the food.

"Whoa, slow down," Marty said with a laugh, petting them while they ate. "That food isn't going anywhere."

Peaches came up to them, sniffing at the kittens curiously. After a few moments, she decided the kittens weren't a threat and went about her business. Marty sat cross-legged on the floor beside the kittens, watching over them. She was simply glad that she had found them and was able to give them some help and relief.

After a few more minutes, Marty checked her

watch and gasped. "I've got to get going!" She placed the kittens back in their box and petted them one last time. "I'll be back soon, but I've got to go for now. Take a nap, sweet things."

As if they could understand her, the kittens curled up together, purring softly, their eyelids already beginning to droop shut. Marty smiled down at them one last time before she hurried to her room to gather her purse, cell phone, and keys. She had a date to meet her mother and sister at Seastar Espresso, and she didn't want to be late.

About ten minutes later, Marty pushed open the door of Seastar Espresso, looking around for Darla and Lori. She spied them at a corner booth by a window and she waved to them before going to the front counter to order a caramel macchiato. Charity had her order ready in no time and soon Marty was joining her mother and sister.

"Hey, you two," Marty said as she slid into the booth and got settled. "What did I miss?"

"Not much," Lori replied, smoothing down an errant strand of her red hair. "Darla was just talking about how her art classes are going at the school."

"They're going really well," Darla said, taking a sip of her coffee. "It's so amazing to watch the kids' eyes light up when they understand a new concept or come up with a brilliant new idea for their art project."

"That must be so rewarding," Marty commented.

"It really is. Who knew I would love teaching kids so much?"

"And to think, this all started with you agreeing to teach at the summer camp."

"That visit to Whale Harbor for Grandma Abby's funeral changed my life for the better," Darla agreed. She smiled a little sadly. "Grandma Abby always knew how to work miracles. Even after her passing she still manages to make my life better."

"To Grandma Abby," Lori said, lifting her mug.

The two sisters echoed her toast and clinked their mugs against hers before taking a drink.

"So, what else is new?" Marty asked.

"Well," Darla said, "I've been helping Rick with some of his boat tours."

Marty felt her jaw drop open. "Are you serious? But... what about your seasickness? You're notorious for getting seasick!"

Darla chuckled. "It's true. Anti-nausea meds help a ton, but I'm also starting to find my sea legs."

"Really?"

"Really. It's actually pretty fun helping him with the whale watching tours."

Lori smiled. "That's wonderful. I think I speak for all of us when I say we never thought you of all people would find your sea legs."

"I know," Darla said with a laugh. "It surprised me too." She took a sip of her coffee. "Marty, what's new with you?"

Marty set aside her mug of coffee, leaning forward. "Well, I found two of the tiniest stray kittens under my front porch today, right before I came over to meet the two of you."

"Let me guess," Lori said with a fond smile. "You took them in?"

Marty grinned. "You know me too well."

"Two new kittens?" Darla asked. "So that makes three cats in your house now?"

Marty felt herself blushing. "I know, I know, I'm officially the crazy cat spinster. But you should've seen them—they were so tiny and they needed a home! I don't know if I'll keep them or give them to the shelter, but I had to take them in for the time being."

"Of course you did," Lori said kindly. "They're lucky that you found them. Other folks wouldn't have been so compassionate."

"Well, I don't know about that," Marty hedged.

"I do," Darla said firmly. "You're a saint, Mar."

Marty laughed. "Hardly. Anyway, they're napping in their little box right now and they've had a good meal, so that's a start."

"As for you being a crazy cat lady spinster," Darla said, "you're not a spinster! You may be a crazy cat lady, but you're not a spinster! There's someone out there for you."

"I don't know," Marty said, twisting her mug around in her hands. "Some people just don't find anyone."

"Don't give up hope yet," Darla replied. "I had no idea when I left New York to visit Whale Harbor that so much in my life would change. Not only did I rediscover my passion for art and discover a love for teaching kids, but I also reconnected with Rick. I couldn't have planned for that, but it happened at just the right moment." She smiled at her sister. "You never know who will come into your life. Or when."

Marty nodded, somewhat encouraged by her sister's words. Still, she couldn't help but think that it was easy enough for her sister to say—Darla took risks. Marty was too worried that letting a guy into her heart would ruin her very stable and very safe life. It wasn't quite the same for her as it was for her sister, so could her sister's words still be true for her?

Lori took a sip of her coffee and then delicately dabbed at her lips with her napkin. "Speaking of men, did you know that Wyatt Jameson bought a space from me to set up shop?"

Marty tensed, knowing her mother's "casual" remark wasn't really so casual. Lori knew how close she and Wyatt had been and, just like Darla the other day, Marty knew that there was subtext in her mother's words. It embarrassed her now, just as hints in that way had embarrassed her growing up. People had often thought they were dating back in the day, and it had always filled Marty with mortification to have to tell them that they weren't dating. Or worse, she would have to stand there like a fool while Wyatt disabused them of that notion.

"Hmm," was all she said by way of response. "Well, that's great for him. I'm sure his shop will be a success."

She took another sip of coffee to cover her embarrassment, not taking her mother's bait to delve into the topic. Thankfully, her mother's cell phone rang at that moment, saving her from having to talk about Wyatt any more. Lori picked up the call and talked for a few moments before hanging up, looking excited.

"Someone wants to see a place I've been trying to sell for a long time," she announced, her blue eyes alight with excitement.

"The house on Windsor Avenue?" Darla asked.

Lori nodded. "The very one. I don't want to miss out on this opportunity, so I said I would show it to them right away. I hate to cut this short, but I really need to get going."

"Of course," Marty said, waving her mother away. "Go get 'em, Mom."

Lori stood, hoisting her purse onto her shoulder. She turned to Marty. "Actually, there is one more thing before I go."

"What is it?"

"I actually have some papers that finalize the transaction that I need to get to Wyatt. I was going to go over right after we finished with coffee, but now I won't have time because I need to show this house. Could you drop it by to him on your way home?"

Marty sat stunned. She knew exactly what her mother was doing: trying to throw her into Wyatt's path and see what would happen.

"Um... can't this wait until Monday?" she asked.

"No, hon, it really can't, I'm so sorry," Lori

replied, fishing the papers out of her bag and dropping them on the table. "I would really appreciate it if you would do this for me."

"Are you sure? I—"

"Thank you so much, sweetie," Lori replied, blowing her daughters a kiss and bustling out of Seastar Espresso.

Marty stared after her, her mouth hanging open.

"I actually have to get going too," Darla said apologetically. "I have a date with Rick. He's taking me sailing and we're having a picnic lunch."

Marty shut her mouth, trying to shake off her surprise and embarrassment about having to go see Wyatt that afternoon. "Aren't the boat tours enough for you?"

"Apparently not," Darla replied with a laugh, standing up. "Okay, I'll talk to you soon."

"Bye!"

Darla left, leaving Marty to stare down at the papers. She sighed, putting them carefully into her bag and standing up. Quietly, she cleared up the empty mugs and carried them to the dirty dish pan that Charity kept out to collect used mugs. Not quite ready to go out and face Wyatt just yet, Marty paused to talk with Charity.

"Hey, how are things going? How's Lucas?" Marty asked.

Charity's delicate features softened at the mention of her adorable five-year-old son. "Lucas is loving kindergarten," she said.

"That's wonderful!"

"And he loves Darla's art classes too. He's becoming quite the little artist."

"Well, I know Darla loves teaching the classes, so I'll pass that along."

Charity's eyes looked a little strained, and her jet black hair was messier than usual. Marty's heart tightened at the sight.

"Charity? Are you okay?"

"I'm fine," her friend said.

Marty arched a brow at her. "Come on, you can tell me."

The tall woman sighed, her brittle smile drooping. "It's... been hard. Divorcing Sid was the right call, but Lucas still asks about his dad and... it's just been hard, you know?"

"Oh, Charity..."

Charity rubbed her forehead. "It's going to be okay in the end. I made the right decision, even if it's hard."

"I'm here for you if you need me," Marty said.

"You can talk to me or come over and just hang out if you need a break."

"Thanks," Charity replied, smiling sadly. Her brown eyes glistened slightly as she added, "I'm lucky to have a friend like you."

"Of course. Anytime."

New customers came in just then, and Charity had to go serve them, so Marty waved goodbye and exited the shop.

As she walked down the sidewalk, her thoughts lingered on divorce. It was so sad and so messy. She hated to see the breakup of dreams and happiness that all couples hoped for when they got married.

Her thoughts turned to Wyatt, and she wondered about his divorce. Had they gotten a divorce because he couldn't settle down? She quickly banished the thought, thinking it was unworthy of her to think that. Besides, divorce was hard.

How hard had that been for him? Was he okay? She really wanted to know how he was, she had to admit to herself.

Well, I'll probably find out soon enough, she thought, looking down at the documents in her bag. *Guess I shouldn't put off the inevitable. It's time to go see Wyatt.*

CHAPTER FOUR

Wyatt grabbed his crowbar, wedging it behind the hideous old cabinetry hanging on the wall and flexed, pulling with all his might. He could feel the veins in his forehead bulging as he strained and, finally, just when he thought he couldn't give any more, the nails in the cabinetry connecting it to the wall popped free and the cabinet thudded to the floor. He stepped out of the way just in time and wiped at the sweat on his forehead, looking at all the cabinets that still remained attached to the wall.

Just a billion more to go, he thought with a groan.

Before he could bellyache about it internally too much longer, Wyatt moved to the next cabinet. Thankfully, this one detached from the wall much more easily than the last one and he grunted in satisfaction as it tumbled to the floor. Tossing the crowbar aside, he hefted up one of the cabinets and walked it out the back door to the dumpster he had rented that was resting in what would be his small parking lot later. He tossed the cabinet in and returned inside for the next one.

The work of getting his shop ready was extremely physical, and he was grateful for all the athletic hobbies he'd had growing up that made it a bit easier now. There was a lot of work to do on the shop—a whole lot—before it would be ready to display dirt bikes and ATVs, but he had a vision and he was confident that he could get the shop to where it needed to be by his opening date.

Inside, he picked up the crowbar and wedged it behind the next cabinet, straining as he pulled. Just as the nails were about to give way he heard someone calling his name.

"Wyatt?"

He turned, hopping out of the way just in time as the cabinet crashed to the floor, to see none other than Marty Sims standing there. He felt his eyes widening and a pleased smile bloomed on his face.

"Well, well, well, if it isn't ol' Marty Sims," he

teased, genuinely delighted—and surprised— to
see her.

"The very same," she tossed back, smiling softly.

Wyatt took her in, noticing how her wavy dark
brown hair fell softly around her shoulders and the
way her eyes glowed honey brown in the sunbeam
slanting through from the front window. She looked,
in a word, stunning, and he was surprised to even be
noticing her in that way.

It's not that weird, he objected internally. *I
haven't seen her in years. Of course I'm going to
notice how she looks.*

"Hey, I'm sorry to just barge in like this," Marty
was saying and he nodded to show he was paying
attention, glad she couldn't read his thoughts. "I did
knock, but I don't think you heard me."

"Over the crashing going on in here? I wouldn't
have been able to. I'm glad you just came in."

He fell silent and so did she, simply standing
there and staring at each other, taking in the changes
of the years that had passed since they'd last seen
each other. He felt the awkwardness of the silence
and cursed himself for not being able to think of
something to say. Marty shifted uncomfortably.

"It's really, really good to see you," he said softly,
opening his arms for a hug.

Marty beamed at him, the awkwardness dissolving as she stepped into his arms and squeezed him tightly. He breathed in the faint scent of lavender on her, and he liked it. He was a little sorry when she stepped away a moment later.

"I actually dropped by to give you these papers for my mom," Marty said, digging into her bag and pulling out a sheaf of papers. "She couldn't drop it by herself and asked that I do it for her."

Wyatt took the papers, glancing through them and nodding. "Oh, perfect, I've been waiting for these. Thanks for bringing them." He looked up at her, smiling crookedly at her. "I'm kind of glad she couldn't come." He felt his cheeks suddenly flame. "Not that I wouldn't want to see her, of course," he babbled, "I just meant—"

Marty laughed. "I know what you meant. It's good to finally see each other again."

"That's exactly it," he agreed with a laugh, running a hand through his hair and shaking his head.

"So this is going to be your new shop?"

Wyatt nodded, looking around at the mess. "I know it doesn't look like much right now, but I have big plans for it."

"Tell me about them. I want to envision the space the way you're going to have it set up."

"There's the interior designer in you talking."

"Of course!"

Wyatt laughed, leading her around the shop and gesturing with his hands. "I'm going to clear out all these tacky old cabinets and then patch the drywall and repaint the whole room."

"What color?"

"I'm leaning toward white—I want it to feel fresh and clean in here, especially since there isn't a whole lot of natural light."

"It'll help showcase your quads and bikes, too," Marty added, nodding seriously and tapping her chin. "White will be like the blank canvas that allows your wares to shine."

"Which is exactly what I want. I'll have the quads lined up here," he said, gesturing to one area of the room, "and the dirt bikes over here. I'm going to build a front desk up by the door and then the back room will be divided into an office for me and an area to restore and repair bikes and quads."

Marty was nodding as he spoke. "It's going to be really awesome when it's all set up."

"I like to think so," he agreed modestly, but he

couldn't help from smiling, knowing he was probably lighting up like a kid on Christmas morning. "I can't tell you how excited I am about this shop. This is the culmination of a lot of years of dreaming and working and saving."

Marty laid a hand on his arm and smiled up at him. "I'm really proud of you," she said simply.

Wyatt returned her smile, surprised at the way his stomach flipped a little at her innocent touch. "Thank you. That means a lot coming from you."

"Well, I don't know about all that..."

"Hey, don't sell yourself short." He stuffed his hands into his pockets and rocked back and forth on his heels. "What about you? I've heard that your interior design shop is doing well."

Marty nodded. "Sand 'n' Things is flourishing more than I ever expected it to," she admitted, smiling quietly. "It's doing all right."

Wyatt shook his head, knowing that she was just being modest. She was so amazing and talented, he had no doubt that Sand 'n' Things was one of the most popular shops in Whale Harbor. He had always known growing up that was destined to succeed, what with her work ethic and her eye for design and style.

"I'd say it's doing more than 'all right' based on

what I've been hearing around town," he commented. "I'm sorry I haven't gotten over there to see it myself—I've been meaning to, it's just..."

"It's just that you're super busy here," she finished for him. "I totally get that. I remember when I was getting ready to open my shop," she said, shaking her head as she remembered back through the years. "The shop was all I thought about, and I put in *so* many hours curating my wares and trying out different setups. Not to mention the nitty-gritty details of getting a business license and funding and all of that."

"It's so much more than I expected," Wyatt admitted. "Being a small business owner is not for the faint of heart."

"No, it isn't," Marty agreed, "but it's so rewarding. It's worth it."

"I think I would feel a little better about my shop if I had your steadiness and dependability," he said thoughtfully. "I know I can do it, but I hate dealing with all the minor details."

"I know what you mean. You'll be great, though."

"Thanks."

"Well, you're welcome to drop by my shop any time. I'd love to show you around."

"I'll make the time," he promised. "I have to see Peaches, at the very least," he teased.

"There it is, the real reason you're coming to visit," Marty joked back. "I knew it was always Peaches."

"Hey, you have a sweet cat," he defended himself, laughing a little.

"I've adopted two more cats back home, Bertram and Macy," Marty said, looking a little sheepish. She raised a hand. "Don't even say it, I know, I know. I've become a crazy cat lady. I was just telling my mom and sister earlier that I'm basically becoming a spinster already."

Wyatt shook his head, his expression turning serious. "You're never going to be a spinster. You're too amazing for that. And far too beautiful."

Marty blinked, her cheeks heating up in a blush. He bit his lip, shocked that he had said that last part aloud, but he couldn't take it back now. Besides, it was so true. Silence stretched between them. This time, though, it was charged with some tension he couldn't quite put his finger on, something electric. He shifted awkwardly, running his hand through his hair again, deeply aware of the elephants in the room —her singleness and his divorce. Thankfully, the moment soon passed.

"Well, I should probably get going," Marty said, hitching her purse up higher on her shoulder. "I know you have a lot of work to get to here and I need to check on my little strays."

"You mean Bertram and Macy?"

Marty blushed again, shaking her head. "No, I found two more strays under my front porch this morning," she admitted. "So, they're staying with me until I find them a home." She lifted a hand again. "I know, crazy cat lady, you don't have to say it."

Wyatt shook his head, amazed at her generosity. "That's not what I was going to say at all. I was going to say it's noble and compassionate of you to take these cats in and find them a good home."

"Oh," Marty said with a blink. "Well... thank you."

Wyatt leaned down and picked up his crowbar again. "It was really good to see you again. We should make time to catch up soon."

"Absolutely," Marty agreed, reaching out to give him a quick one-armed hug. "We'll talk soon," she said over her shoulder as she headed for the front door.

Wyatt watched her leave, admiring the way her curls bounced when she walked and then shook his head. What was happening to him? Marty had always been his best friend—the person he looked up to most in the world, but now he was seeing her in a new light, seeing her as a woman and not just a friend, and he didn't quite know what to make of it.

Slow down there, cowboy, a voice in his head said sternly. *You just got out of a nasty divorce. Are you really going to think about dating already?*

Wyatt frowned, his jaw clenching as he began working on the next stubborn cabinet. There was probably no point in even thinking about Marty in that way. After his divorce, he was pretty much damaged goods and he wouldn't be surprised if she could never see him as a viable prospect. The thought filled him with a deep sadness, but he wasn't one to let things keep him down for long.

Maybe she doesn't see me that way now, but it doesn't mean she never could, he thought firmly.

He knew that for that to be a possibility, he would have to work hard to show her that he was the kind of man she could depend on. Someone steady and responsible and worth her time. Sure, he had made mistakes in the past, plenty of them. But that didn't meant that he couldn't build something real and lasting with someone now. His divorce had been a trial by fire, but it had taught him a lot about what he wanted in the future and the kind of man he wanted to be. He knew that he had a lot to give to the right woman, that he wanted something real.

He just hoped that Marty would be able to see it that way too.

CHAPTER FIVE

Darla blew her auburn hair out of her eyes and focused on her painting. She was so close to finishing it that she could almost taste it, but it wasn't quite there yet. It was still missing something. She dabbed her paintbrush into one of the daubs of paint on her palette and added a few brushstrokes to one of the hands she had painted, giving it added dimension and depth.

She was painting a couple holding hands, but it was zoomed in on just their hands, showing the fingers interwoven together, the play of strength and intimacy found in such a simple gesture. She was in love with it—every time she looked at it, it reminded her of Rick and the happiness she had found with him. In a way, this painting was a symbol of their young love, growing and deepening all the time.

A few brushstrokes later, Darla smiled, a sense of satisfaction filling her. The painting was finished. She felt it all the way down to her bones. She set aside her paintbrush and simply stared at it, taking in the two hands holding one another, one masculine and strong, the other delicate and feminine. It was beautiful, breathtaking even, and she was beyond pleased with the way her vision had come into reality.

Lightness filling her, she stood up and began cleaning her paintbrushes in the sink of her studio. Ever since she had moved to Whale Harbor, her creativity had been flowing nonstop, and sometimes she felt like she could barely keep up with all the ideas in her head waiting to be painted onto the canvas.

That's a good problem to have, though, she thought as she scrubbed at the paint sticking to the bristles of the paintbrush.

Indeed it was a good problem to have. Who would have thought that her sleepy hometown would provide her with the exact space she needed to be her most creative self? Unlike the rat race in

New York, there was never any pressure on her here when it came to her work. She could paint whatever she was inspired to paint, instead of trying to guess what would sell best or impress the art critics in order to advance her career.

On top of her painting, she was still teaching art classes at the school, which she absolutely adored. As she helped them explore their artistic talents, it fed and nourished her own creative spark, keeping her in touch with her roots and adding to her ideas all the time. The children were so full of creativity and originality that they inspired her all the time. No, one thing was certain—teaching at the school was only serving to make her a better artist. Who would have thought? Not Darla, at least not at first, but here she was.

Setting her now-clean paintbrushes into a can to dry, Darla glanced at the clock hanging on the wall of her studio and gasped. She had been so immersed in the process of painting that she had entirely lost track of the time, and now she was running behind. She was meeting Rick at his boat for an evening date, and she didn't want to be late.

Hurrying into the bathroom attached to her studio, Darla fussed with her hair a little, disentangling the curls and fluffing them up, then swiping on some lip gloss from her purse and refreshing her mascara. Pleased at the results, she blew a kiss into the mirror, laughed at herself for her silliness, and grabbed her purse to run out the door. Her outfit wasn't the cutest—she was wearing her painting overalls and a paint-stained t-shirt, but she didn't have time to change. It would be what it was, but she had a feeling Rick wouldn't mind. He always made her feel like the most beautiful woman in the world, even when she was wearing grungy painting clothes or pajamas she'd owned since college.

Darla parked her car by the dock and hurried down the wooden boards toward Rick's boat. He looked up from where he was working on the deck as she approached and lifted a hand in greeting, walking over to help her board the boat.

"Hey, gorgeous," he said, grabbing her around the waist and pulling her close.

"I don't know about that." She laughed.

"I do," he said, seriously, tucking her hair behind her ear and lowering his head to kiss her deeply.

When they broke apart, he looked a little unsteady on his feet, the same as she felt, but it had nothing to do with the boat's gentle movements beneath their feet and everything to do with that earth-shattering kiss.

"Wow," Darla whispered, looking up at him, knowing she was probably blushing hard.

"Wow is right," Rick said, blinking a little. He gave her a lopsided grin. "Somehow I still haven't gotten used to the amazing experience that is kissing you. I hope I never do."

Darla snuggled closer against his chest, loving the feel of his arms around her and breathing in the scent of his cologne. "How's your day been, love?"

"Better, now that you're here."

Darla swatted at him. "And before I arrived?"

"It's been fine. The tours went well today—we saw three whales while we were out, so the tourists were very pleased."

Darla leaned back to stare at him. "That's amazing! Three? Really?"

Rick nodded. "I know, I was over the moon about it."

"As you should be."

Rick stepped back and began unwinding the rope that was attached to the dock. "How's your stomach doing? Are you going to be okay?"

Darla nodded. "I should be fine. I took some anti-nausea meds just in case, though."

Darla had been working to combat her seasickness since she'd moved back and was slowly but surely finding her sea legs. Still, they were going on a date tonight, out on the water, and she didn't want to risk a bout of seasickness ruining the moment. That would be more than unfortunate. Besides, she was loving spending more and more time out on the water. The beauty of the scenery never failed to move her, and it was providing her with endless inspiration for her paintings.

Rick steered the boat away from the dock and headed for the open water, steering the boat skillfully. Darla leaned against the railing and watched him work, loving his casual competence and the way his muscles rippled beneath his t-shirt as he steered the boat.

"What? Do I have something on my face?" Rick asked after a few minutes.

"What?"

"You've been staring at me for like five minutes," Rick said with a chuckle.

Darla blushed, smiling. "Honestly, I was just thinking about how handsome you are. I don't think I'll ever get used to it. I can't believe that I, Darla Sims, am dating *the* Rick Maroney. I mean, high school me would never believe it!"

Rick burst out laughing at that. "I don't know about 'the' Rick Maroney, but I can tell you high school Rick is freaking out about the fact that he's dating the mysterious and artistic Darla."

Once they got far enough out onto open water, Rick came over and joined her at the deck, coming up to stand behind her and wrapping his arms around her waist. He rested his chin on the top of her head and they stood staring out at the softly rippling water. Overhead, the sun was beginning to set and the sky was splashed with magnificent pinks and oranges. The sun, a giant orange orb, was sinking toward the horizon, which was laid out in front of them as far as the eye could see.

"I don't know how we got so lucky," Darla said softly, leaning against Rick's chest.

"Hmm?"

"To have found one another again," Darla explained.

"I know. I think about that all the time."

"And, thanks to you, I discovered how much I love teaching art to children."

"I can't take credit for that."

Darla twisted around in his arms to face him. "Of course you can! You're the one who had the idea for me to teach a few classes to the summer camp kids and that changed everything."

"Well, when you put it that way..." Rick said with a teasing smile. "I guess I should get some credit, huh?"

Darla swatted at him playfully. "You're such a tease. Anyway, it makes me super excited to teach our future kids all about art."

Darla felt Rick stiffen, becoming tense. His jaw hardened and a muscle twitched in his jaw. Darla furrowed her brow, stunned by the sudden change in his entire demeanor.

"Rick? What just happened? What's wrong?"

Rick sighed, looking away from her and out at the water. He let go of her and went to stand against the railing. Darla watched him for a moment, stunned at how suddenly he had become entirely aloof and distant. She rubbed her arms, as though to ward off a sudden chill.

"Rick?"

Rick ran his fingers through his dark blond hair and finally turned to face her, folding his arms. "It's just... I actually never thought I would have kids. I never saw it in the cards for myself, and... I'm not sure that it's something I want."

Darla felt her stomach drop and she knew her

eyes were wide and hurt. She struggled to keep her breathing steady as her mind reeled.

Stay calm, she told herself. *Stay calm and just hear him out.*

"Really?" she asked, trying to keep her voice casual, but it came out as more of a squeak. "You've never wanted kids?"

Rick shook his head, pursing his lips. "I never saw myself as the type to have kids, and that definitely solidified while I was in Alaska. You know, that's just not the type of environment where having kids would be smart. I guess I just never revisited the idea after I moved back here."

Darla nodded slowly. "And there's no part of you that thinks you might want kids?"

Rick shrugged. "I don't know. Not really? I'm not one hundred percent sure, I guess."

Darla swallowed hard, feeling tears threatening to rise. "I see."

Rick's expression softened and he reached out a hand, gently lacing his fingers through hers.

"Hey," he said, his voice turning soft. "We don't have to have the answers to this question right now. This is an issue we can shelve for the time being."

Darla swallowed again, nodding. "You're right. We don't have to have all the answers right now."

"I love you so much," Rick said, smiling gently at her. He tugged softly on her hand, pulling her toward him until he could wrap his arms around her. "And that won't change. We're going to be just fine."

Darla nodded against his chest, glad she could bury her face against him and not have to meet his light brown eyes at the moment. The tears were still there, threatening to fall, and she didn't want to cry about the issue they'd just decided to put on hold for the time being.

Still, even as their conversation drifted to other things, Darla's mind returned again and again to the fact that there was something so important that she hadn't known about Rick. She had thought their relationship was so solid, but here was a gaping hole, a problem that they hadn't addressed.

They had been in the honeymoon phase for so long, she had almost forgotten that real life was still there, waiting for them.

And boy, had it hit with a vengeance.

Darla knew she had met her dream man. Rick was everything she wanted and more in a relationship. Still, they had just uncovered a serious issue about which they did not agree. Having kids was just something Darla had never foreseen as an issue. It was something she had always wanted for her own life, and now Rick was saying he probably didn't want children.

Could their relationship survive this disagreement? And more importantly, could Darla build her dream life with her dream man?

CHAPTER SIX

"Bye, everyone," Marty said, hitching her purse onto her shoulder. "It was so good seeing all of you!"

Rick, Darla, and Lori looked up from the table where the remnants of their card game were still laid out.

"It was good kicking your butt at Uno too," Darla said sweetly, her eyes gleaming with mirth.

"Oh, hush, I let you win," Marty teased.

She walked over to the table and kissed her mom on the cheek and then waved to Darla and Rick. "I've got an early morning at the shop tomorrow, so I'm going to call it a night."

"Thanks for coming over, dear," Lori said. "Drive safely."

"Will do."

Marty gave everyone one last wave and then let herself out of the house and headed toward her car. As she drove, she reflected on the game night she had just enjoyed with her family and Rick. It was great to spend an evening with her loved ones—the family was finally coming together again after being splintered for so many years. First when their father had separated from their mother, but then the relationship between Darla and Lori had been so strained for so long, but it was healing now too. A few months ago, an evening like this would never have occurred, and Marty was deeply grateful for the progress her family had made in becoming closer and more tight-knit.

And it had been nice to have Rick there too. Marty loved watching him and Darla interact, although tonight they had seemed a little strained. It hadn't been anything overt, but Marty had picked up on an undercurrent of tension between the two of them that made her uneasy. She wondered what was wrong but knew that it wasn't her place to ask. If Darla wanted to talk about it, she would. Hopefully it was nothing big and, for her sister's sake, she hoped they passed through it soon and got back to solid ground. Darla deserved nothing but happiness, in Marty's opinion.

And, tension or no, Marty had still loved watching Rick and Darla together. It was clear how deep their bond ran, and it made her think all over again about how she wanted someone like that in her own life. Someone for game nights. Someone to spend time with when she got home from her shop in the evenings. Someone to do all the little things in life with.

Marty sighed, parking her car in her driveway and slowly getting out. Her cozy home waited for her, but she didn't want to go in just yet, because she knew it was empty. No one waited for her inside.

That's not true, she scolded herself. *There's Peaches and the new stray kittens. You have more company than most.*

And it was true, but somehow cats weren't quite the same as having a lover, a companion to spend her life with.

Oh, stop feeling sorry for yourself, that little voice in her head whispered. *You have a good life.*

Her self-scolding wasn't doing anything but making her feel worse, so she tried to let it go. Grabbing her purse, she got out of her car and locked it, then headed up the front steps of her house and let herself inside. Immediately, Peaches bounded over to her and began rubbing against her legs. Marty hung her purse carefully on its hook in the hall closet and then bent down to pet Peaches.

"Come on, you sweetheart," she cooed. "Let's go check on our new kitten friends."

Peaches trailing behind her, Marty stepped into the kitchen and checked the box where she was keeping the two stray kittens. They were curled up together, tails entwined, fast asleep, their tiny chests rising and falling with each breath. Marty checked their food and water bowls, pleased to see that there was still some left in each bowl, and she made a mental note to call the shelter to get them placed into a home soon.

She really couldn't have three cats in one house. It was just too many. Right?

"Now, time for your food, my sweet little babies," Marty cooed, going over to the feeding dish for Peaches.

She opened up three tins of wet cat food and scooped them out onto the special plate she kept just for feeding her cats. As Peaches ate, she sat on the floor cross-legged, petting Peaches and admiring the softness of her fur. Petting Peaches always soothed her ruffled feathers, and tonight they were ruffled just a bit, probably from her worries about Darla and Rick. That and her wish for a companion of her own.

Finally, when Peaches was nearly halfway through eating her food, Marty rose to her feet and padded down the hallway to her bedroom. She undressed, putting on her favorite silk pajamas with cats printed all over them, then went into the bathroom to wash her face and do her nighttime skincare regimen. It was a ten-step program, rather too long, but Marty didn't mind. She liked the familiarity of the routine, even though Darla laughed at her for it. Darla used a basic face wash from the grocery store and called it a night, but Marty liked taking her time.

She hummed while she went through her skincare regimen, allowing herself to be soothed by the familiar steps. When she was finished, she went into the kitchen to make herself a cup of Sleepytime herbal tea. Peaches rubbed against her legs while Marty brewed her tea, making her smile.

"You're such a good kitty, you know that? Mommy loves you so much."

Peaches purred, as if she could understand what Marty was saying.

Tea in hand, Marty went back to her bedroom and was just settling into bed with an interior design magazine when she heard a faint meowing coming from outside her window. She paused, straining to hear, wondering if it was one of her cats, but no, the sound was definitely coming from outside the house. Peaches jumped off Marty's bed and trotted to the window, craning her orange head to see outside the window. That convinced Marty. There was definitely a cat outside the house, and it sounded like it was in distress.

Not even waiting to put on shoes, Marty raced down the hallway and out the front door. The meowing was growing louder. She hurried across the yard and looked up into the tree that was outside her bedroom window where she was shocked to see an adult calico cat stuck on one of the branches.

"Oh, you poor baby," she breathed. "Here, kitty, come here," she called, reaching toward the cat.

The cat shifted on the branch but otherwise stayed where it was, likely too afraid to try and make its way down to her. It was too high for Marty to reach, and she wasn't the climbing type herself. She quickly ran through some options in her head, then raced to the garage to grab a small stepladder she kept folded up there. She returned to the tree and opened the stepladder, climbing up and reaching toward the cat.

"Dang it," she muttered. The stepladder was still too short to reach the little animal.

She eyed the branch above her, wondering if she could pull herself up onto it. But then how would she get back down? She was just about to reach for the branch when a voice startled her so much that she almost fell off the stepladder.

"Marty?"

She jumped, whipping around and wobbling on the stool as she caught sight of Wyatt, of all people, standing on the sidewalk in front of her yard.

"Do you need some help?" he asked.

Marty could feel her cheeks flaming red. She was out in her bare feet in cat pajamas, and all she wanted to do was shrivel up in embarrassment. She wished the ground would give way beneath her stepladder so that she could disappear, but no such chance encounter occurred to rescue her. Wyatt was walking across the yard to her. The moonlight overhead showed that his features were creased in concern.

"What's going on?"

Marty pointed up to the cat stuck in the tree. "This cat needs help, but I can't reach it. I'm too short, and this stepladder is the tallest thing I have to stand on."

"Here, let me see if I can reach it," Wyatt said, reaching out a hand to help her off her perch.

He climbed up and was just barely able to reach the cat, who hesitated at first.

"I'm not going to hurt you," Wyatt murmured. "Come on, there's a good girl," he said as he picked up the cat and came down the stepladder.

Marty reached for it, and Wyatt surrendered the calico.

"Oh, you poor thing," she said, stroking the cat. "It's shaking."

"Poor little thing was probably scared half to death. Is it yours?"

Marty shook her head. "No, I heard meowing outside my window and came outside to investigate. I suppose I'll have to take it in for the night and then see if I can find its owner tomorrow."

"Do you need anything?"

Marty huffed a laugh, shaking her head. "No, I've got plenty of cat food and kitty litter. This little girl should be just fine for the night."

"It's really kind of you to take her in until you can find her a home."

Marty shrugged. "I can't very well leave her out here to fend for herself. I mean, she got herself stuck in a tree, after all." She petted the cat again. "I'd better get her inside. Want to come in for a minute?"

"Sure. I haven't seen Peaches in ages."

Wyatt followed Marty into the house, where Marty got some food for the cat. The other cats came up to it cautiously, clearly not sure about this stranger in their territory, but they warmed up quickly enough and soon welcomed it without fear. Peaches was rubbing up against Wyatt's legs, purring so loudly it made Wyatt laugh aloud.

"Looks like she still remembers you," Marty said with a smile.

"Looks like it," Wyatt agreed, bending down to pick Peaches up and snuggling her close.

"Thank you so much for your help," Marty said, leaning against the counter and trying to ignore the fact that she was still standing there in her cat pajamas. "I don't know what I would've done without you."

"I'm just glad I was taking a nighttime walk at just the right time and place," he replied, scratching Peaches between the ears.

"You'll have to come by and see how the cat is faring tomorrow."

Wyatt looked disappointed. "I'd love to, but I can't. I'm going to Yarmouth to help my dad out. Plus

I've got to transport a couple of quads they restored that I'm going to be selling in my shop. I really wish I could."

Marty nodded, disappointed as well. Their eyes locked, and suddenly the room felt too small. Marty was all too aware of Wyatt's nearness and she felt electricity zap through the air between them. From the slight flush in his cheeks, Marty wondered if Wyatt was feeling it too.

"I'll come by after I get back, though," he said hurriedly.

"Yeah, that would be great." Marty's words came out in a rush, too fast, and she bit her lip.

"Well, I should probably be going," Wyatt said, putting Peaches back down on the floor.

Marty walked him to the door. "Thanks again."

"No worries."

Wyatt gave her a wave before stuffing his hands into his pockets and ambling down her driveway. Marty watched him for a moment, her heart beating fast, before locking the front door behind him and leaning against it. She couldn't believe that after all these years she *still* had a crush on Wyatt Jameson.

He might be single now, but that doesn't mean he's right for you, a voice in her head whispered.

Wyatt was an adventurous guy, always doing

new things and jetting off on the spur of the moment. He wasn't the type to settle down and she needed to remember that. Even though it hurt she promised herself then and there that the next time she saw him she would view him only as a friend—it was time to let this silly crush go, once and for all.

CHAPTER SEVEN

"That's it, keep on backing up," Frank called to Wyatt from his position guiding the trailer up to the back of his shop.

Wyatt kept his gaze glued to the rearview mirror, following his father's signals as he backed the trailer up toward the back garage door of his father's shop in Yarmouth.

"Almost there, almost there, and... stop," Frank called.

Wyatt put his truck into park and then shut off the engine before climbing out of the truck to join his father. It was a gorgeous Sunday, all blue skies and no clouds, the weather unseasonably warm for September, a reminder that summer had not been so very long ago. Frank stood with his hands on his hips, nodding in approval over his son's parking job.

"Ready to load 'em up?" he asked.

Wyatt nodded. "I'm excited to get them back to Whale Harbor."

He had come to Yarmouth to take a couple of quads that he and his dad had restored to sell back in his new shop in Whale Harbor. He was grateful to still get to work with his dad in this way. They had spent so many years working together in his father's shop, and it had been a bit of a risk to branch out and start his own shop, but he was excited about the prospect.

Frank climbed onto one of the quads, revving it up and driving it carefully up the ramp into the trailer Wyatt had rented. Wyatt climbed onto the second quad and did the same. In no time at all they had both quads loaded and secured in the trailer.

"Son, I just want you to know how proud of you I am," Frank said as they exited the trailer and closed up the back door.

Wyatt smiled. "Thanks, Pops. That means a lot coming from you."

Frank nodded, folding his arms and leaning against the trailer. "How does it feel to be opening up your own shop?"

"It's a big undertaking," Wyatt admitted. "Sometimes I wonder if I've bitten off more than I can chew, but I watched you run your shop for years and I'm confident that I can do it too."

"So am I. You're smart as a whip, son, I've always known that about you." Frank smiled at Wyatt, his eyes warm. "Besides, I'm only ever a call away, plus our shops are going to be working together and sharing resources as needed. Business is booming, and your second location in Whale Harbor is simply needed. There's no way it won't be a success."

"Folks did need an option closer to Whale Harbor," Wyatt admitted. "What with the dunes in Cape Cod being so close. Speaking of, I'm going to a quad competition in Cape Cod in October."

"Oh, the annual October Showdown?"

Wyatt nodded. "Yup, that's the one."

The October Showdown was a competition where the best dune riders around competed for a trophy. Wyatt had competed a few times before and he was looking forward to this year's competition. It was always a fun time and he had the added bonus of getting to catch up with old friends.

"So how are things going in Whale Harbor?" Frank asked. "Miss Yarmouth yet?"

"You know I love Yarmouth," Wyatt responded.

"That being said, it's been good to be back in my hometown. Even though it's where I grew up, it feels "new" in a way, like I'm getting a fresh start."

"Fresh starts are good." Frank looked up at the sky, seeming to be thinking Wyatt's words over. "How have you been doing, son? Really?"

Wyatt knew his father was asking about Helen, his ex-wife. He closed his eyes for a moment as pain washed over him. "I've been doing okay, Dad. Really."

"Yeah?"

Wyatt thought about it, then nodded again. "Yeah. It's not like divorce is ever fun or easy, and I know that's certainly been the case for me. But Helen and I have kept things amicable, and there's no ill will on either side. That's better than a lot of folks going through divorce have it."

It hurt that Helen had chosen to leave him, but he didn't harbor any blame or ill will toward her. They'd been growing apart for a long time. Sometimes marriages just didn't work out, even when both parties cared about each other.

"At least there were no kids involved," Frank said. "That would make things so much messier."

"Agreed. That would've been a nightmare."

Frank nodded, his gray eyes compassionate.

"Well, since you've been back in Whale Harbor, have you run into Marty? I remember she was your best friend growing up."

"As a matter of fact, I have seen her a couple of times."

Frank smiled. "She was such a great girl growing up. I remember being grateful the two of you were friends." Frank eyed him. "You know, what I never understood is why you didn't pursue her."

Wyatt pursed his lips, not sure how to answer his father. "I mean, I just didn't see her that way. She was like a sister to me." He didn't add that his feelings in that regard had certainly changed.

"Hmm. Is she seeing anyone?"

"Not that I know of," Wyatt admitted. "She's... very careful about who she lets into her life, especially when it comes to dating. My 'here and there' nature probably wouldn't suit her anyway." Wyatt blew out a breath, pulling a face. "Not to mention the fact that I'm a divorced man. She probably thinks I can't sustain a long-term relationship or something like that."

Frank looked at him sternly. "Now, don't go putting words in her mouth. That's not fair to her."

"Sorry. Just saying what I really think."

Frank sighed, putting an arm around his son. "I

know your path hasn't been easy, son. Everyone has things they wish had ended up differently—you're divorced, but your life isn't over."

"Sometimes it feels like it is, at least when it comes to love."

Frank squeezed Wyatt's shoulder, his gray eyes kind. "I know it feels that way, but try to keep yourself open to the possibilities. You never know what new thing is going to come up in your life."

"That 'new thing' could be a bad thing," Wyatt pointed out.

Frank gave him a playful shove. "I meant good things and you know that. You've got to focus on what makes you happy and go after that."

Wyatt sobered, nodding at his father's words of wisdom. "I'll try to do that. Thanks, Dad."

Frank clapped him on the shoulder, then pulled him into a bear hug. "That's my boy."

Wyatt hugged him back, grateful to have a father that openly showed affection instead of some 'stiff upper lip' type of dad. They stepped apart and Frank checked his watch.

"Do you have time for a bite to eat before you hit the road?"

"Patty's Diner?"

Frank grinned. "Where else?"

Wyatt's stomach grumbled in anticipation at the thought of Patty's famous hamburgers with fries and a chocolate shake. "I always have time for Patty's Diner," he said with a grin. "Come on, we're wasting daylight, and if I don't get a burger and fries in me in the next twenty minutes, I'm not going to be a happy camper."

Frank laughed. "Way ahead of you, son. Let's go."

CHAPTER EIGHT

Marty shifted her shopping basket to the other arm while she stared at the shelves full of decorative items. She was at Magnolia Street Home Goods picking up some things she needed in order to finish the fall-inspired wreath she was making. She thought it would be fun and festive to hang on the door of Sand 'n' Things, but she still needed to finish it.

"Hmm..." she murmured under her breath, surveying the myriad options.

Would pine cones look good? She liked the texture and interest they would add, but they seemed a bit more associated with winter time than fall. There were some decorative acorns in the next bin, though, which made her eyes light up with excitement.

Those would look so cute against the fake orange and yellow leaves I've already picked up, she thought, reaching for a bag of the acorns and tossing them into her basket. She wandered down the aisle, considering and rejecting a few other options before deciding to pick up some brown gingham ribbon to make a bow on the top of the wreath. Satisfied that her wreath was going to turn out beautifully with the items she had picked out, Marty headed toward the cash registers.

As she walked toward the front, she decided on the spur of the moment to make a quick detour into the candle aisle. She loved smelling all the different scents—it was something of a little indulgence she allowed herself every time she came to Magnolia Street Home Goods. She wandered down the aisle, picking candles at random, lifting the lids, and inhaling their scents. She nearly swooned over a candle that smelled exactly like baking sugar cookies, but ultimately put it back. The next candle was a deep orange and it smelled of cinnamon and pumpkin spice. She kept sniffing the candle, unable to put it back and finally added it to her shopping basket.

That will smell nice in the shop, she thought,

already planning to have it burning the next day when she opened up Sand 'n' Things.

Pleased with her soon-to-be new candle, Marty approached the cash register and began unloading her shopping basket.

"Did you find everything okay?" the cashier asked.

She was a bored-looking teenager, probably a junior or senior in high school, who was chewing gum loudly and tapping out a text on her phone, not bothering to look up at Marty. Marty held back a smile at how obviously bored the cashier was, remembering what it was like to be that age. Sure, she would never have acted like that, but she knew it was all part of the teenage phase.

"I did, thank you," Marty replied politely.

The cashier began scanning her items and placing them into a plastic bag.

"That'll be twenty eighty-five," the cashier said, already pulling out her phone to check a text message.

Marty slid her card into the card reader, waiting for it to accept the payment.

"Thank you so much," Marty said, taking her receipt from the cashier.

"Have a good day," the cashier mumbled distractedly.

"Marty?"

Marty turned around to see Wyatt walking through the sliding glass doors of Magnolia Street Home Goods. Her heart, rather treacherously she thought, began beating harder at the sight of him. He looked good with his sandy hair a bit wind-tousled and wearing a gray t-shirt that subtly highlighted his muscular frame. Marty could feel heat rising in her cheeks at the fact that she was even looking at him that way and mentally scolded herself.

He's just a friend, he's just a friend, he's just a friend, she chanted to herself, but it wasn't working very much. Her pulse refused to slow down.

"Wyatt! Hi!" she chirped, blushing harder at the way her voice sounded a little too eager. She swallowed, forcing herself to take a deep breath. "What are you doing here?" She made a show of looking around the shop. "This doesn't really seem like a place you would shop."

Wyatt quirked up an eyebrow and folded his arms, giving her a teasing grin. "And why not, may I ask? I am a man of refinement and taste."

Marty burst out laughing at that and Wyatt put on an expression of mock offense. "How dare you laugh at me, Marty Sims. I'll have you know that just last week I purchased a vegetable, so I'd say I'm pretty grown-up and refined, if you ask me."

By now Marty was wiping at her eyes from too much laughter. "Oh, stop," she said when she could speak. "You know what I meant."

"I do," Wyatt agreed with an easy grin. "I know this isn't my usual scene. I just got back into town and I'm running a few errands."

"Nice! What have you been up to?"

"I was just at the hardware store picking up some supplies to shine up the quads I just transported from my dad's shop."

"Oh, cool. Did they get here all right?"

"All in one piece," Wyatt said with a nod. "They're running just fine but they could use a polish up."

"Nice. So, how does Magnolia Street fit into your errands for the day?"

Wyatt looked around at the store, his expression a little intimidated. "Well, I was thinking it might be nice to pick up a few things for my new place. My house is pretty bare bones right now—I don't really have much of anything in there."

"That makes sense," Marty said, nodding. "What kinds of things did you have in mind?"

"I'm not sure. Some pots and pans. Maybe a lamp."

Marty burst out laughing again and Wyatt pulled a face at her.

"Come on, what are you laughing about now?"

"It's just, that's not much of a decorating plan," Marty pointed out. "You must have quite the 'bachelor pad' look going on at your house."

"I don't think I have a look of any kind going on right now. Like I said, it's pretty bare bones. I have a bed and... not much else. Which," he added, a touch defensively, though his eyes were twinkling, "is really all I need."

Marty shook her head at him which made him laugh. Her interior design mind was already whirring a mile a minute with ideas for his house.

"A bed alone does not a home make," Marty intoned, and Wyatt chuckled, raising his hands in surrender.

"Well, that's what I've been telling myself, because I'm pretty much hopeless at all this decorating stuff. I know that must seem crazy to you, Miss Interior Designer, but not all of us have your gifts." He paused, looking at her. "You know, maybe you could come over and take a look, give me some ideas on how I could decorate the place."

Marty laughed, then stopped when she realized he wasn't joking. A ripple of excitement ran through her at the idea, but she chewed her lip, still a little uncertain. Was spending more time with Wyatt really a good idea? If she could just keep it at the friends level, it would be fine, but her heart seemed to keep betraying what her mind ordered. Every time she saw him all of her plans to just be friends seemed to fly out the window and she always seemed to forget that he wasn't the type of guy to settle down.

"I don't know..."

Wyatt's face fell and Marty felt horrible.

"...if you could handle living in a home that looks as good as I'm going to make it," Marty finished, and Wyatt burst out laughing, his face relaxing into a huge smile.

Marty relaxed, too, glad to see that he wasn't hurt anymore.

Besides, she told herself, *Wyatt's a busy guy. He's probably never going to actually follow up with me about this. No need to worry.*

"Want to help me right now? You can help me pick out a lamp or something."

Marty shook her head. "I would never start buying things without making a plan first. Get your pots and pans but don't buy anything decorative yet."

"Sir, yes, sir!" Wyatt said, saluting her, which made Marty roll her eyes.

"I've got to run another errand, but I'm sure I'll see you around town soon enough," she said.

Wyatt gave her a look. "Yeah, when you come over to help me make a plan for my house."

"Right," she said, still not really believing he was actually going to follow up about it later. "Okay, see you later."

Marty headed out of the store, putting her purchases into her car and then climbing in. She started the car, flinching a little when the radio blared at her. She had been jamming out on the way to Magnolia Street and had forgotten to turn down the radio before shutting the car off. Volume at a decent level, she drove to the supermarket and parked.

She took her time inside the store. Something about grocery shopping soothed her. It always had. She liked the neat aisles with so many options and she liked knowing that by shopping she was filling her larder at home and keeping everything in her life running smoothly. She pushed her cart down the aisles, picking up a salad for dinner and a bottle of wine, as well as some bread, cheese, cereal, and a roast chicken.

Before she could forget, she headed down the pet supplies aisle and picked up some special treats for her cats, as well as some more cat food. With four cats in the house, she was running low on food and treats.

She finished up her shopping and headed home, cooing to her cats as she walked through the door, her arms full. Peaches got in her way, trying to rub against her legs.

"Give me a minute, Peaches." She laughed, setting down her bags on the kitchen counter and scooping Peaches up. "Hello, baby, did you miss me? Who's the sweetest cat? Is it you?"

Peaches purred as though she could understand the words, and Marty reached out with one hand to open up the bag of treats. She gave one to Peaches, which made the cat purr even harder. The two kittens mewed from their box, and the calico cat meowed loudly, clearly having smelled the scent of the treats.

Marty laughed, sprinkling some treats into the kittens' box and then giving a couple to the calico. While they were busy with the treats, Marty checked all of their food bowls and water bowls, refilling them as needed. Glad that her cats were taken care of, Marty made a mental note to ask around about the calico cat and see if she could find its owner. If not, she needed to look into finding it a good home. And not just for the calico, she needed to find homes for the stray kittens too. They couldn't live in a box on her kitchen floor forever.

She was just beginning to unload her groceries when she felt her phone buzz in her pocket. She pulled it out, surprised to see a text message from Wyatt. She unlocked her phone to read the full message.

WYATT: Hey, how does coming over to my place tomorrow work?

Marty blinked in surprise. He *had* followed up, and so quickly too. She quickly tapped out a response, her heart beating faster as she typed, a little flutter of excitement in the pit of her stomach.

MARTY: Sure, sounds good. Around 4?

WYATT: That's perfect. Just so you know, my house puts the 'humble' in 'humble abode,' so... no judgment, lol.

MARTY: I wouldn't dream of it. Scout's honor.

WYATT: Were you even a scout?

MARTY: Not relevant. ;) Hey, can you text me your address?

Wyatt did, and she thanked him, then slid her phone back into her pocket, willing her heart rate to slow. As she continued to unload her groceries, she found herself murmuring under her breath, "We're just friends, we're just friends, we're just friends..."

And, just as before, her mantra did nothing to dispel the fluttering excitement in her belly about seeing Wyatt the next day.

CHAPTER NINE

Rick lugged the bucket of dead fish down the employees-only hallway at the Marine Center. He was headed to the seals exhibit. It was feeding time.

The odor of fish wafted up from the bucket, awful and terribly pungent, but Rick was used to it. As he walked, the bucket bumping against his leg, he thought about Darla and the conversation they'd had on his boat the other day.

Pausing in front of the back door to the seals exhibit, he set the bucket down and pulled out his ID badge to unlock the door. Inside the seals exhibit, the sounds of seals barking assaulted his ears, which only grew louder as they realized their food had arrived. Bouncing and waddling, the seals descended on him, making him smile. He realized as he did so that it was the first time all day that he had really smiled, but the realization didn't surprise him. Things hadn't been so good since he'd taken Darla out on the boat.

One of his favorite seals, affectionately named Chumbo for his rather impressive weight, stared up at him with liquid eyes, waiting impatiently for his fish.

"All right, all right." Rick chuckled. "Food's coming!"

He tossed a fish into the air and Chumbo caught it, gobbling it down. Rick went around, feeding all the seals, but he made sure to save one extra fish for Chumbo. He shouldn't, and he knew it, but he loved Chumbo so much and he didn't think a treat would hurt just this once.

In a few more minutes the seals scattered, realizing the bucket of fish was now empty, heading back to their places on the rocks to lay out. Chumbo waited a moment longer, staring up at Rick hopefully.

"That's it," Rick said. "There's no more, see? Besides, you already had an extra fish!"

Chumbo snuffled and then waddled away, flopping over on a rock and closing his eyes in a blissful post-dinner nap. Carrying his now empty bucket back out of the room, Rick closed the door firmly behind him, waiting until he heard the lock engage. He headed down the hallway to the supply room where he stowed the bucket and peeled off his gloves, tossing them in the trash, then wandered into the office to grab the closing time checklist. He marked off the seals as fed on the checklist.

As he scanned the list, seeing what he needed to do next, bits of his conversation with Darla on the boat floated through his mind.

Really? You've never wanted kids?

He could still see the disappointment and shock on Darla's face as he told her that he'd never seen himself as a potential father, had never envisioned a life in which he had kids. They'd agreed to table the conversation for the time being, but it had continued to hang over them ever since, an unspoken specter looming between them, coloring each interaction with its choking hands.

Rick sighed, running a hand through his hair in frustration. Was he really so wrong for not wanting kids? It was just something he'd never really thought about, not something he'd ever particularly desired.

But I should've known that she would want kids, he thought, feeling a dull ache in the pit of his stomach.

The worst part was, he felt like a complete fool.

How could he have allowed himself to fall head over heels in love with this woman without having such an important conversation first? What if this was an issue they couldn't work through? Could he really just let Darla walk out of his life?

Never.

Not after having experienced what it was to love her. Just the thought of losing her made him feel almost physically ill. He swallowed against the nausea threatening to rise and once again saw Darla's troubled face in his mind's eye. How could they have not discussed the issue of having children earlier on in their relationship? Was it possible that he would lose her if they didn't come to a solution? Rick shuddered at the thought. That was the last thing he wanted. He wouldn't—couldn't—lose her. He wouldn't be able to bear it.

"Rick? You okay, man?"

Rick blinked, looking up from the checklist he'd been staring at with unseeing eyes. He focused his gaze and saw Jordan, one of his coworkers and friends, standing in the doorway to the office.

"What? Oh, yeah, I'm fine."

Jordan folded his arms, leaning against the doorway to the office and looking skeptical. "You sure? You seem... out of it."

"Just lost in thoughts, I guess," Rick said with what he hoped was a casual shrug.

"Yeah? Those thoughts don't seem to be good ones."

"What do you mean?"

Jordan's brow furrowed as he watched his friend. "You were scowling and you just seem really upset."

Rick sighed, blowing out his breath and setting the checklist down. "You got me. Yeah, I'm not really okay right now."

Jordan nodded, his lips quirking to the side in sympathy. "Do you want to talk about it?"

"I don't want to burden you with it, but thank you."

"Come on, man, what are friends for? I wouldn't have asked if I didn't mean it," Jordan assured him.

"You're really sure?" Rick asked cautiously.

"I really am. What's up?"

Rick sighed again, rubbing at his tired eyes. "Well, Darla and I were talking the other day and she brought up having kids. I freaked out a little, because I've never pictured myself having kids, and I know that it hurt her. I just... I don't want to lose her over this. I don't know what to do."

"Wow..." Jordan said slowly, shaking his head. "That's a tough one."

"You're telling me," Rick said, giving a mirthless laugh. "It's a hopeless case."

Jordan held up his hands. "Whoa, I didn't say that, and I wouldn't go that far. It *is* a tough case, but I don't think it's hopeless."

"You don't? Then what should I do?"

"I can't tell you that, honestly. I don't really have any advice for you—not on a topic this important— but I will say you've caught me by surprise."

"What do you mean?"

"Well," Jordan said, looking thoughtful. "I'm kind of surprised to hear that you don't want kids. I've seen you interact with the summer camp kids and the kids who come here to the Center. I guess I've just always seen you as the type that would be a natural dad."

Rick blinked, surprised. "Really?"

Jordan nodded. "Yeah, you're really good with them."

Rick chewed on this bit of information, stunned. He could barely picture himself as a father, but knowing that Jordan saw him as a father type actually did help a little. The fact that someone he trusted had confidence that he would be a good dad helped in a way that he hadn't expected.

"Thanks, man," Rick said slowly. He shrugged.

"I'm still not sure myself that I would be a good dad, but... I really don't want to lose Darla, and it seems like having kids is really important to her." He swallowed hard. "It seems like having kids would make her happy, and... the only thing I want in this life is to make Darla happy."

"Are you saying what I think you're saying?"

Rick shrugged. "I wouldn't go that far yet. Let's just say I'm open to the possibility. She really wants children so maybe I could make the space in my life to want children too." He looked over at his friend, feeling better than he had in days. "Thanks for working through this with me. It's helped a lot."

Jordan laughed aloud at that. "I didn't even do anything! You worked out this dilemma all on your own."

Rick chuckled sheepishly. "Maybe so, but sometimes you need to have someone repeat your own words back to you so you can hear how silly—or selfish—they sound. It was silly of me to risk losing my relationship with Darla over this, when I'm not necessarily opposed to having kids—I'd just never really thought about it. I had a bad knee-jerk reaction when she brought it up and it's been haunting us ever since."

"Well," Jordan said, a smile playing around his

lips, "telling you when you're being silly is something I'm always down to do."

"I'll bet," Rick said dryly, smiling back. "I'm sure you'd be more than happy to perform that particular service."

"Hey, what are friends for?"

Rick laughed, slapping Jordan on the back and pulling him into a bear hug. "Seriously, thanks, man. You helped me work through things that had gotten all snarled up in my own mind. I needed some help untangling the royal mess that was going on up there."

"I'm happy I could help," Jordan replied. "Anytime you need to talk, I'm here for you."

"Thank you," Rick said sincerely.

"Now," Jordan said, reaching for the checklist Rick had discarded, "let's get back to work. Those sharks aren't going to feed themselves!"

CHAPTER TEN

Wyatt tightened the screw on the part he was working on, grunting a little as he tightened it all the way. He set his screwdriver down, wiping at his forehead with the back of his arm and looked at the dirt bike he was working on in his garage at home. Sure, he had plenty to keep himself busy at his shop, but he always liked to have a personal project going on at home—he liked to keep his personal restorations separate from his work ones. This current home project was coming along nicely, if he did say so himself. He estimated that he would have it completed in the next couple of weeks and he couldn't wait to take it out for a spin when it was finished. There was nothing quite like riding on a quad or a bike that one had restored with one's own hands.

Whistling to himself, he grabbed a rag off his workbench and began polishing the leather seat of the dirt bike, trying not to think about the fact that any minute Marty was going to arrive. The thought made something in his stomach flutter, which made him feel like a nervous schoolboy—embarrassing in the extreme. There was no reason to be feeling this way around his lifelong best friend, or at least, that was what he kept telling himself, but so far it hadn't helped to calm the butterflies that insisted on taking off every time he thought about her.

He was just checking his watch to see that it was 4:00 when he heard a car drive up his driveway. He looked up, seeing Marty put the car into park and then climb out. She must have just come from her shop, because she was wearing professional black palazzo pants and a silk blouse, her wavy hair swept up into a loose bun. Those pesky butterflies in his stomach flapped wildly about as he watched her come toward him and he couldn't help but notice how good she looked. How had he never noticed that before in all their years of being friends? It was like he was seeing her with brand new eyes for the first time. He tossed the rag back onto his workbench and stood up.

"Marty! Right on time, as always," he said, offering her what he hoped was a casual smile. He was glad she couldn't hear his thoughts or hear the butterflies still flapping wildly in his stomach.

"What can I say? I pride myself on my punctuality," she tossed back with a grin. "Is this a bike you're restoring?"

Wyatt nodded, stroking the buttery leather of the seat. "Yup. It should be finished in a couple of weeks."

Marty walked around it, surveying it seriously. "That's just so incredible to me. I honestly don't know how you understand how all the parts work together. It blows my mind."

Wyatt shrugged modestly, though his heart warmed at her simple words of praise. "It's actually not that complicated once you've done it a couple of times."

"Hey, don't sell yourself short. You do incredible work."

"Thank you. Let's just hope the rest of the folks in town think that—it would really help the success of my shop!"

Marty chuckled. "I'm sure your shop is going to

be wildly successful. No need to worry about that." She paused, pursing her lips. "I do know what it feels like to worry about the success of one's shop, though. Opening up a small business is a gamble and it honestly feels so scary when you're first starting out."

Wyatt blew out a breath, glad she understood. "Right? It's nerve wracking! Sometimes I can't sleep at night just thinking about what will happen if my shop fails."

"Which doesn't actually do you any good," she said softly. "I know—been there, done that."

"And now your shop is flourishing."

Marty smiled at him, her brown eyes just exactly the color of honey in the slanting sunlight that filtered into the garage. "It is," she admitted, unable to hide the pride in her voice. "It took a long time to get there, though. Don't give up."

"I don't plan on it," Wyatt promised. "I'm going to give this everything I have." He looked back down at his bike and got an idea. "Oh, by the way—have you ever gone to a quad race event?"

Marty shook her head. "Nope, not once."

"Well, there's one this Friday that I'm competing in. It's not as big as the October Showdown, but it'll still be really fun. Want to come?" He held his breath, waiting for her response. Suddenly, it mattered a lot to him that she said yes.

Marty hesitated, biting her lip as she thought it over. "I never really thought of going to a quad race—it's not my usual scene, but you know what? It could be fun. I'm in."

Wyatt felt a goofy grin blooming on his face. He was ridiculously pleased about the fact that she was going to come to his race and he knew he would have to do some soul searching later on about why that was. He was starting to wonder what it would feel like to be more than friends with Marty, but he wasn't quite sure how to cross that line. Maybe this event would be a good start.

"So, are you going to show me this humble abode of yours?" Marty asked, cocking her head to the side and smiling at him.

Wyatt nodded, but he hesitated. "Remember how I told you when we were texting that it was super humble, right? So, no judgments?"

"I promised I wouldn't judge, and I meant it," Marty said with a soft smile.

"Okay, then, let's go," Wyatt said, taking a deep breath. He was suddenly a little nervous to show Marty, an accomplished interior designer, his barren living quarters.

He opened the door in the garage that led into the house and let Marty step inside first. The kitchen was just off the garage, which looked fairly normal since she couldn't see at first glance that practically every cupboard was empty inside. Marty wandered in, looking around herself with obvious interest. She ran a hand along the countertop absentmindedly as she looked around at the bare walls, not a piece of artwork or a clock or even anything hanging on his refrigerator in sight.

From the kitchen, he led her into the living room, which held only a foldable camping chair and a TV that sat on the floor. He cringed at the sight of it, waiting for Marty to say something, but she only smiled at him and looked around the room.

"There's great light in here," she commented. "That will be really nice once you get this room set up the way you want it."

He could have kissed her on the spot for finding the good in a very bleak situation, but he restrained himself, simply smiling at her happily. After the living room, he showed her the bedroom, which consisted of a mattress on the floor and a suitcase splayed open that held a jumble of his clothes. At least he could say that he had proper sheets and a duvet on the bed—that at least spared him from some embarrassment. A quick tour of the bathroom completed the circuit of his small home and they headed back into the kitchen. To his surprise, Marty hopped up on the counter to sit and something about it made him smile. There was that fun streak hiding just below Marty's cautious surface that he loved so much.

"Okay, doc," he said, stuffing his hands into his pockets. "Give it to me straight—is it a hopeless case? What's the diagnosis?"

Marty burst out laughing at that.

"Seriously, though," he continued. "I know I put the 'bachelor' in 'bachelor pad' in this case."

He immediately wished he could take his words back as soon as he said them. Why, oh why, had he brought up the fact that he was a bachelor? It only served to remind him of the fact that he was a divorced man. Even more so, it reminded of the fact that he was single and she was single... and that fact had changed the dynamic of their relationship, even if neither of them was actually bringing it up. There was no way she wasn't aware of the sparks that kept flying between them, right?

To his relief, Marty simply smiled and said, "It's not as grim as you think! I can spruce it up and make it more homey while still keeping it true to your personality. I promise I won't bury the couch in a million throw pillows or hang up frilly lace curtains."

Wyatt pretended to wipe his brow in relief. "Phew! Glad we're on the same page there. So, what ideas do you have?"

"Well, for starters, simply getting some basic furniture would be good. You know, a bed frame, a couch, and maybe a chair or two. A stand for your TV. Oh, and an actual shower curtain."

"What's wrong with mine?"

"It's a liner! That goes inside your shower. You're supposed to have a decorative shower curtain on the outside so that it isn't completely see-through," Marty said, cracking up.

Wyatt pretended to jot down some notes. "Got it, got it. Okay, this is all good. Keep the tips coming."

"Well, the furniture you pick out will help us know how to decorate the rest of your house. It will help us to pick out things like lamps and artwork, the things that make a home feel lived-in and cared for."

"You do realize that I'm going to need your help shopping for furniture, right?"

"And I'm happy to do it," Marty promised.

"That's a relief."

"Hey, I can't have you buying some monstrosity

of a couch and ruining all my plans to make this space livable," Marty joked.

"Noted. No monstrosities allowed," he teased back.

Marty nodded, looking around the kitchen. "And maybe once you're settled in, you can get a pet. Those always make a house feel like a home."

"Maybe. Speaking of pets, how are the stray cats doing?"

To his surprise, Marty's cheeks flushed a little. "Uh... well... they're not strays anymore, because... I took them in."

"Like for keeps? I thought you said four was too many."

Marty groaned and covered her face with her hands. "I know! It *is* too many, but I couldn't find them any other homes and by then I was super attached to them, so..."

"So you decided to keep them all," Wyatt finished for her, grinning broadly.

"I know, I know," Marty grumbled. "You can call me a crazy cat lady. I already know what I am."

"I wasn't going to say that!" Wyatt insisted, holding up his hands. "Actually, I think it's sweet. Those cats are lucky they stumbled into such a good home."

"Well, thank you. They're all doing really well and, luckily, they all get along, so that's a plus."

"Definitely a plus," he agreed. "I'm going to have to come over sometime and say hi to all the cats. Peaches and I are old buddies, but I need to get to know your three new cats."

Marty hesitated, and Wyatt could almost read her mind. He had always been the type to swing in quickly before disappearing again. That had been their relationship for the past several years, even before he was married. He knew it had to have been hard on Marty, who craved stability. He felt himself shriveling up inside a bit at the thought that Marty didn't trust him because she couldn't depend on him to actually stick around, and then he remembered what his father had said about going after what he wanted and not letting the past define him. And he was realizing more and more what he wanted had been right in front of him for so long: Marty.

"Hey," he said softly, waiting until she met his eyes. "I just want you to know... I know I've been all over the place in the past and that you couldn't depend on whether I'd be around or not, but that's all changed now. I bought this home and I bought the shop and I'm putting down roots. I'm here to stay."

Marty nodded slowly and her eyes became liquid

with tears as she processed the fact, but she quickly blinked them away, giving him a watery smile. He ached to reach out and pull her close, but he held himself back, simply enjoying the moment they were sharing.

"It's good to have you back," she said simply. "Whale Harbor just wasn't the same without you."

Wyatt felt himself beaming, but he didn't care. Her words meant everything to him.

Marty slid off the counter. "Okay," she said, clapping her hands in a businesslike manner. "Let's do another walkthrough, and this time we'll start making serious notes about what to do with your house. Sound good?"

Wyatt nodded, unable to hide his smile. "Sounds good. Lead the way, captain."

CHAPTER ELEVEN

"Oh my goodness, who's the most precious baby?" Marty cooed at the calico cat, which was rubbing up against her legs while she put on her mascara in the bathroom. "Is it you? Yes it is, you cutie."

The cat purred, making figure eights around her legs and Marty had to pause doing her mascara so as not to smudge it. She laughed a little, looking down at the still-nameless calico cat.

"I need to name you," she said aloud, considering the sweet cat down by her feet. "I'm sure when the time is right, it will come to me."

The cat blinked up at her with its big green eyes as if it knew exactly what she was saying. Marty smiled down at it and then returned to swiping on her mascara. She was almost finished getting ready for the day and it tickled her to no end that the calico cat had followed her around as she'd gotten out of the shower, gotten dressed, and was now doing her makeup. The cat was super cuddly and loved to follow her around, which made Marty think she might be a good candidate for leash training.

"We'll try one on you just as soon as I finish getting ready," she promised, winking down at the cat.

Marty put her mascara away in her makeup organizer and then put on a pair of classy silver drop earrings before surveying herself in the mirror and pronouncing herself ready for the day. True to her word, she walked to her closet of organizing supplies and pulled out the leash she usually used for Peaches.

She crouched down beside the calico, strapping her into the harness and waiting to see how she would react. To her delight, the cat stood there calmly, blinking up at her as if to say, "See? It's all good, no big deal."

Marty clipped the leash onto the harness and began walking down the hall to test the cat. Like a natural, the feline trotted along beside Marty, following when she turned back down the hall and made her way toward the kitchen.

"You're a little natural," she cooed, taking the leash and harness off for the time being.

The two kittens and Peaches began meowing at her as she entered the kitchen, clearly indignant that they hadn't yet been served breakfast, which made her chuckle.

"Calm down, calm down," she murmured, still laughing softly. "You act like you're all starving to death!"

Reaching into the cabinet where she kept the dry cat food, Marty filled up each of their bowls and then refreshed their water bowls. The cats all raced toward their food and got down to business, while Marty crouched beside them and petted each of them in turn. They purred a bit, but otherwise ignored her while they chowed down. Marty stood, contemplating her own breakfast. She desperately needed a cup of coffee, but a look in her cabinet told her she was almost out.

"Well, no problem," she said aloud, looking down at the calico cat, which had left its food and was once more by her feet. "How about I take you for a little field trip, huh? I need some coffee and I bet you would love to take a jaunt through our little town."

The cat meowed up at her and Marty laughed.

"I'll take that as a yes," she said, reaching down to scratch between the calico's ears.

Grabbing her purse and keys, Marty once more attached the harness and leash to the calico cat and let herself and the cat out of the house, locking the door behind them. She walked the cat to the car and opened the door for her to jump inside first. The calico settled herself on the passenger seat while Marty buckled into the driver's side, and soon they were off, driving slowly toward downtown Whale Harbor.

Even with the increased traffic in the downtown area, the cat showed no signs of distress. In fact, she got to her feet to peer out the window with evident curiosity at the passersby. Marty parked in front of Seastar Espresso and got out, the calico following her on the leash. She walked the cat to the door and pushed it open, allowing the calico to enter with her as the delicious aroma of freshly brewed coffee greeted them.

"Look, Mom! A cat!" Lucas chirped, racing around the counter where he had been standing beside Charity to hurry over to Marty's side. He stopped, looking up at her, his eyes huge and wondering. "May I pet it, please?"

Marty nodded. "Of course!"

Lucas immediately sat down cross-legged on the floor and began petting the calico's head ever so gently, then scratched between her ears. The cat arched her back luxuriously, clearly enjoying the attention, which made Marty smile.

"What a cute cat," Charity said, coming around the counter too and giving Marty a quick hug. "Is she new?"

Marty nodded. "I found her in a tree outside my house. No one came forward to claim her when I asked around, so I guess she's part of my family now."

"Lucky cat," Charity said with a smile. She looked down at her son fondly, who was now immersed in rubbing the calico's belly. "Lucas, honey, remember that you have to leave for school in the next couple of minutes."

"Okay, Mom," Lucas said distractedly. The cat was purring and licking at his hands.

"How are things going for you?" Charity asked.

"Oh, you know," Marty said, giving a little shrug. "It's same old, same old. Just plugging away at the day to day. You know how it is."

Charity speared her with a knowing look, barely holding back a wicked grin. "Really? I wouldn't have thought that seeing Wyatt again would exactly classify as 'same old, same old'."

Marty could feel her cheeks warming under Charity's close scrutiny. "We're not 'seeing' each other," she insisted. "I mean, he asked me to help him decorate his house, but that's it."

"He asked you to help decorate his house?" Charity asked, raising an eyebrow. "Now I'm *really* not convinced that there isn't something going on. What guy asks for help decorating his house?"

"Umm... someone who knows what a good interior designer I am?"

"Uh-huh, sure," Charity said, looking entirely unconvinced.

In truth, Marty wasn't entirely convinced that nothing was going on either. She had been feeling some major vibes from him the other day at his house, vibes that he might be into her. And she couldn't lie and say that she hadn't been trying to quash the very real interest she still had in him. The only problem was that she still wasn't sure that he was a good match for her. Sure, she liked him and cared about him a lot, but he was... Wyatt. Spontaneous, ramshackle, always on the go, adventurous Wyatt. Surely a match between the two of them would never work.

Marty decided it was time to change the subject. "How are things going with your divorce?"

Charity's face fell into serious lines. "Well, it's divorce, so it's hard," she admitted, keeping her voice low enough that Lucas wouldn't be able to hear her. "I mean, it's going as well as can be expected, but there's so much pain that comes along with it, you know?"

"I'm so sorry," Marty murmured, reaching out and laying a hand on Charity's arm.

Charity forced a smile and gave a tiny shake, as though trying to clear away the topic. "It makes me think about Wyatt, though."

"What?" Marty said, blinking in surprise.

"Going through my divorce," Charity clarified. "Just because he split with his wife, it doesn't mean he wasn't a good partner in that relationship or that he can't be a good partner in a future relationship."

"I see..."

Charity gave her a sad smile. "I know I gave my marriage my all, but it still wasn't enough to save it. I would hate to be stigmatized because of my divorce. I would hope people won't judge me for it. By that same token, I won't judge or make assumptions about Wyatt because of his divorce."

Marty nodded slowly, really taking in Charity's

words. "That's a really good point," she murmured, suddenly having a lot of food for thought.

Had she been making assumptions about Wyatt because of his divorce? If she was being honest with herself, yes, she had been. She had seen it as a sign that he was too flighty to settle down, that he couldn't handle being in a committed relationship. She hadn't really said it in so many words, even to herself, but that had been the underlying assumption, and now she felt horrible about it. How could she have judged him like that just because he'd gotten a divorce? She knew Wyatt. She knew what a good guy he was, and here she'd been assuming things about him just because he and his wife had split. And, she realized, she had assured herself that it would be foolish to allow herself to feel anything for him because of those assumptions. The thought made her feel a little sick. How could she have been so foolish?

"Wyatt invited me to a quad race this Friday," she admitted, her voice quiet now too.

"Really? That sounds like fun."

"I mean, I didn't know if I should go, but after what you said, it's got me reevaluating things."

Charity smiled at her kindly. "That's why I brought it up. I know you've got some reservations about Wyatt, and his divorce probably hasn't helped that, but he's a good guy and he doesn't deserve to be stigmatized because he got a divorce."

"So you think I should go?"

Charity nodded. "Of course! I think you'll have a blast, and I bet it would mean a lot to Wyatt. He wouldn't have invited you if he didn't care about you showing up."

Marty smiled at her, grateful for her friend's advice, as well as the reminder that divorce didn't have to define a person. Wyatt was someone who had constantly seemed to be on the move, always looking for adventure. He'd never been one to stick around, and she'd taken his divorce as further proof of that. But Charity had reminded her that it wasn't fair to judge him for his divorce. Even more than that, Wyatt himself had told her that he had changed and was putting down roots.

She sighed, wishing she could look into the future and see how everything would work out. That way she could save herself from making a mistake if Wyatt hadn't really changed.

That's just your cautious self talking, said the little voice in her head. *No one can see the future. You may have to take a risk here.*

"Can I get you anything to drink?" Charity was

asking. "Lucas, honey, it's time for you to go to school."

"Aww, man," Lucas groaned. "But I was having so much fun with Marty's cat!"

"I know, sweetheart, but you've got to get going or you'll be late. You can play with Marty's cat another time."

"That's right," Marty assured him. "We'll have to set up a playdate or something."

Lucas beamed at that and jumped up, grabbing his mom for a quick hug and then running out the door. Charity watched him go, smiling and shaking her head at his antics.

"Sorry, did you say you wanted something to drink?"

"I hadn't said anything, but I would love a latte, please."

"Sure thing, coming right up!"

Charity bustled behind the counter to start whipping up Marty's drink and the calico cat rubbed against Marty's legs. She scooped the cat up and snuggled her close. As Marty buried her face in the soft fur, she wondered once again if it was safe to take a chance on Wyatt. No one, no crystal ball or fortune teller, could tell her if it was a sure bet with him. She would have to take a chance.

The question was, would she be brave enough to do it?

CHAPTER TWELVE

Darla's stomach grumbled as she drove down the streets of Whale Harbor toward her sister's house. She and Marty were going to make dinner together and have some much needed sister time. Darla had been looking forward to it all day—things with Rick were still rocky and she needed a night of relaxation and warmth to help soothe her ruffled feathers. Pulling the car into Marty's driveway, she smiled at the sight of two kittens watching her from the window.

Grabbing her purse, she climbed out of the car and walked up the front steps, knocking lightly on the front door. A moment later, Marty answered it, wearing an understated black jumpsuit with an apron on over it.

"Darla! So glad we could do this tonight," Marty said, smiling warmly. "Come on in."

"Ugh, I've been needing this," Darla replied, setting her purse down on the credenza in the entryway.

The kittens that had been watching her from the window sauntered into the entryway, rubbing up against her ankles. "Hello there," Darla said, reaching down to pet them. "Aren't you all so teeny tiny and cute?"

"I know, aren't they?"

"Do these two have names yet?"

"I was thinking Bertram and Macy."

"Bertram and Macy... I like it," Darla said, reaching down to scoop them both up and cuddling them close. "How has it been having four cats?"

Marty blushed a little, but smiled. "I know, it's crazy to suddenly have four cats, but it hasn't been bad. I mean, I'll be honest—I haven't enjoyed cleaning out four litter boxes, and I haven't liked having to buy so much cat food, but it's worth it. They're all sweethearts and they all get along so well."

"That's great! Sounds like Peaches isn't jealous?"

"Nope! I think she enjoys the company."

"That's wonderful," Darla said, smiling as she

put the kittens back down. Her stomach grumbled again. "So, what are we making for dinner?"

"I was thinking we could make lemon parmesan baked chicken with some roasted potatoes and an arugula salad on the side. Does that sound good?"

Darla nodded, already salivating a little. "At this point, a stale granola bar sounds good."

Marty laughed. "That hungry, huh?"

"Starving!"

"Well, we can't have that. Hold on, let me get you some crackers and brie to snack on while we make dinner."

Darla beamed at her sister, ever the gracious hostess. "That sounds perfect. Mar, you're too good to me."

"And don't you forget it," Marty teased, going into the kitchen and pulling a wheel of brie out of her refrigerator, then going to the cupboard to pull out some artisan crackers. She arranged them on a plate and set them on the counter so that they could graze while they prepared the meal.

"So," Darla said, going over to the sink and washing her hands, breathing in the citrusy scent of Marty's grapefruit hand soap. "What can I do to start helping prepare?"

"Want to help me scrub and peel the potatoes?

The oven is already preheating for the chicken and the potatoes."

"Sure thing."

Marty bustled over to her pantry and returned with a sack of golden baby potatoes, which she handed to Darla. Before getting to work, Darla grabbed a cracker from the tray on the counter and popped it into her mouth, chewing gratefully on the food. After one more cracker with some brie, she reached inside the sack and began pulling out potatoes and holding them under the tap water, scrubbing them with a potato scrubber Marty handed her.

"So," Darla said, scrubbing at a potato, "how's your project going at Wyatt's house? Is it all decorated yet?"

"Oh, not even close," Marty replied, squeezing fresh lemon onto two chicken breasts. "I mean, there's just so much to do. When I went over to his house, he had a camping chair, a TV, and a mattress. That was basically it."

"Talk about a bachelor pad."

"No kidding! It's essentially a blank slate."

"Which makes it all the more fun for you," Darla pointed out.

"Exactly!" Marty smiled. "It's going well. I went

through his house and came up with a list of things he needs to shop for right away—like a bed frame and a couch, etc etc—and then we'll tackle the little decorative touches that take a house from feeling bare bones into a cozy home."

"Well, he's in good hands—he only got the best interior designer in Whale Harbor."

"I'm pretty much the only interior designer in Whale Harbor," Marty said, rolling her eyes, "so that isn't too difficult."

"Hey! Don't sell yourself short. Even in a bigger city, he would still have been lucky to land help from you." She finished scrubbing another potato and set it aside, eyeing her sister. "So, it sounds like things with him are going well?"

Marty blushed, biting her lip. "The *project* is going well. Don't even think about asking about anything else."

Darla raised her hands in surrender. "All right, all right, you can't blame me for being curious."

Marty blew out a breath and tossed the used up lemon in the trash, then leaned against the counter. "Okay, fine. Yes, there are some major vibes going on between me and Wyatt, but I don't know what it means. Plus, it seems like other people are picking up on it."

"Well, it sounds like a confusing situation. I'll respect your privacy, though." Darla reached for another potato, thinking about Marty's situation. "I will say this, though... just let things play out, okay? That's what led me to moving back to Whale Harbor and getting with Rick. So, sometimes it's okay to just have faith and see what happens, rather than trying to control or predict the situation." She eyed her cautious, security-loving sister. "I know that's easier said than done, though."

Marty blew out a breath, shaking her head. "You said it," she agreed. "It's so hard to feel like I can't predict what's going to happen. It just goes against everything in my nature, but I'll try to remember what you said, especially considering that that worked out so well in your life."

Darla reached for the peeler and began peeling the potatoes over the trash can, working steadily and setting the finished potatoes onto a cutting board.

"Speaking of your life, how are things with Rick? I don't mean to pry, but things have seemed... off... between the two of you lately, especially the other night."

Darla sighed, her stomach squeezing a little at the new topic. She chewed the side of her lip, wondering where to begin. "Well... before the game night Rick and I had a date night out on his boat. While we were out on the water, I made some comment about our future kids, and he totally tensed up! When I asked him about it, he said that he'd never thought he would have kids, that it was just not something he'd planned to have in his life."

"And you've always wanted kids," Marty pointed out softly.

"Right." Darla shook her head, closing her eyes for a moment. "He said that we didn't have to figure it all out right then, but I'm worried about it, you know? We *have* to talk about it again at some point, and what if we can't come to some kind of agreement about what to do? What if this comes between us and ruins things? I mean, Mar—he's the love of my life, but what if I can't have my dream life with him?"

Marty wiped her hands off and came over to Darla, wrapping her arms around her. "Oh, Darla..."

Darla returned the hug, feeling tears threatening at the corners of her eyes. She sniffed, gently disentangling herself from the hug and continuing to peel potatoes so she would have something to do. She focused all of her attention on the potato she was peeling to try and keep herself from crying.

"Maybe he'll change his mind," Marty said as she

sprinkled parmesan over the chicken breasts. "You never know."

"Maybe," Darla agreed, but she had little faith in her response. "I just wish I could know for certain what was going to happen."

"I know how you feel," Marty said sympathetically. "Remember what you told me, though. You have to just let things play out and hope for the best without trying to control the situation."

"Did I say that?" Darla joked feebly.

"You did," Marty said firmly, "and it's good advice. Can you picture your life without Rick?"

Darla thought about it, trying to imagine a life where Rick wasn't a major part of things, and she simply couldn't. "No," she said finally. "I can't."

"And can you picture your life without kids?" Marty asked softly.

Darla set her potato down on the cutting board, feeling as though the wind had been knocked out of her. She closed her eyes, trying to picture a different life than she had always imagined. She pictured a life with Rick by her side, but where they grew old alone, just the two of them in Whale Harbor. A life where there was never the pitter-patter of tiny feet against the wooden floors of their home, where she never snuggled her own baby close. Again, she wasn't sure if she could do it. No matter what, though, Marty had given her a lot to think about.

Just then, Bertram leaped at the garbage can, flicking at a piece of potato peel that leaned on the edge. He missed, backflipping in the air and landing on his little feet, looking astonished at that turn of events. His antics broke the solemn mood of the moment and Darla found herself chuckling in spite of herself.

"He's a silly one, isn't he?" she asked.

"Oh, all cats are silly. The best part is that they think they aren't, though. I love it."

"I know! They act like they have such dignity and then they do the stupidest things imaginable," Darla said, laughing aloud now as Bertram chased his own tail, then, hearing their laughter, lifted his little nose into the air and walked crisply out of the room with all the dignity in the world.

Darla shook her head. "What a character."

"Oh, he's got loads of it," Marty agreed. "Come on, let's get these potatoes cut up and roasting in the oven."

Together, the two sisters quickly chopped up the potatoes and got them buttered and seasoned, then popped them into the oven. Marty threw together the arugula salad while Darla set the table, the two sisters chatting easily all the while. While she worked, though, Darla couldn't help but think back to Marty's questions earlier.

Could she picture her life without kids, even if she got to spend it with the love of her life? She still didn't have the answer, and she knew it was going to hang heavy on her mind for a long time to come.

CHAPTER THIRTEEN

"And you can have that ready to ship by tomorrow?" Wyatt asked into the phone.

"Yes, sir, expect the shipment to arrive in the early afternoon."

"Perfect!"

Wyatt ended the call and fist pumped the air. He already had a couple of quads and dirt bikes to sell for his shop, but those were pieces that had been restored. Tomorrow afternoon, his first shipment of brand new quads and dirt bikes would arrive for the shop. The shop itself was looking far different than it had a couple of weeks before. It was now freshly painted with wide open spaces for the quads and dirt bikes to be displayed, plus a brand new front desk for him to check out people's purchases. His displays of bike and quad accessories, as well as the obligatory cash register candy stock, was all ready to go. He should be ready to open for business in the next couple of days.

Wyatt shook his head, still unable to believe that he was finally at this stage in the process of opening his own business. There were times it seemed this day would never come, but here it was, and the feeling of satisfaction was unbelievable. He ran a hand along his brand new front counter, looking at the new iPad he'd purchased to serve as the register. Everything looked spic and span, and he was beyond proud of the work he'd done. He'd certainly poured his blood, sweat, and tears into this shop.

As he walked around the shop, taking it all in, Wyatt thought about his life. Years ago, he'd pictured that at this point in his life he would be all settled down, maybe even with a kid or two, but he clearly hadn't been as ready to do that as he would have wished.

I could have had that, a small voice whispered in his head, and he winced.

It was true, though. He could have had that life. Helen had wanted children, but she didn't want to raise them alone, and he was gone so much with his dirt biking events. She had told him again and again that he wasn't present enough in their relationship, but he hadn't really listened, thinking that he was present plenty of the time. That decision had cost him everything in the end. They had grown apart as he was away all the time and finally things had just fallen apart.

And it was my fault. Mine.

Sure, it took two to make a marriage work, but Wyatt knew things would likely have been different if he had listened to his wife and been more willing to settle down, more willing to prioritize her as the number one most important thing in his life. She had wanted a quiet life with a man who had a regular schedule and a safer hobby, someone who could be relied on. Instead, he'd continued focusing all his energy on quad and bike racing, and he hadn't considered how his consistent absence had made her feel.

Well, he knew now, and he had learned the hard way.

I don't ever want to make my significant other feel that way ever again.

And it was true. His divorce, though amicable, had been a trial by fire and it had taught him so much about what he wanted for the future—both the man he wanted to be and the kind of relationship he wanted to have. He had learned that a life didn't have to be filled with constant, breakneck activity to be meaningful, that he *could* settle down and be happy.

That realization made him think of Marty, someone who had been on his thoughts almost constantly since he had returned to Whale Harbor. Marty, like his ex-wife, craved stability. He knew that he didn't exactly fit that mold, but he was learning how to do that, and he was determined not to mess things up with Marty. They were building on his friendship and he liked the direction things were going between the two of them. Maybe, if he kept showing her that he could be relied on, their friendship would deepen into romance, into something real.

"I can't believe I wasted so much time not being able to see what was right in front of me all along," he murmured to himself, running a hand through his hair in frustration.

Marty had been there practically his whole life, and it had taken a divorce and his life falling apart for him to see the gem that had been right in front of him the whole time. It made him feel almost sick to think of the fact that she could have been swooped up by someone else, but that was by the merest chance. Sure, she didn't date much, but Marty had the creativity and gentleness that many men would feel fortunate to have.

Why didn't I go after her before? he thought, shaking his head at his own stupidity.

But, a moment later, it occurred to him that maybe he hadn't been ready before. He had been too immature, too wild and reckless. Marty would never have gone for him before, and he couldn't blame her. He had needed to go through some hard life lessons to realize how to be a better partner. And, now that he was learning those lessons, he finally felt ready to be the man that Marty could hopefully see herself settling down with.

I didn't deserve her before, he realized, and the epiphany stung a little. *But now? I'm still not sure if I'm good enough for her. She's an angel, but... but I want to try.*

And it was true. There was nothing he wanted more—not his shop, not biking, not his racing events —than to be the kind of man that would deserve Marty's love. He knew it with his whole heart, and the realization filled him with joy and determination to do his best.

She was coming to his race this week to support him, which made him super excited, but he quickly realized he was far more excited to see her than to actually compete, something his younger self would never have felt. He hoped that she would be able to feel that from him on Friday, would be able to see that, even though he was competing, he wasn't the same Wyatt she had grown up with all those years ago.

Wait for me, Marty, he wished, closing his eyes. *I'm coming for you.*

CHAPTER FOURTEEN

Darla sank onto the couch, taking in a luxurious breath as she leaned her head against a throw pillow. It had been a long day of teaching art classes at the school and, while she had loved every minute of it, she was exhausted. She closed her eyes, wiggling her toes contentedly and thought back through the day. The kids were learning about watercolor painting, and it had been fun to teach them the principles of watercolor and what a powerful medium it could be.

As she lay on the couch, Darla thought about a sweet interaction she'd had with one of her students, Alice, earlier that day. Alice was a delightful second grader with a gap between her front teeth and the biggest brown eyes she'd ever seen. Alice had taken naturally to art lessons and she constantly surprised

Darla with her latent talent. Earlier that day Alice had come up to her to show her the watercolor she was making of her father's boat. It had Alice and her father manning the boat, sailing off into a sunset, and Darla had been delighted with it.

"This is beautiful," Darla had told the little girl, who had beamed shyly. "You're really good at painting!"

"It's because you're a good teacher," Alice had said back, giving her a hug out of the blue. "When I grow up, I'm going to be an artist like you. Thank you for being my teacher!"

Darla had been too choked up to do anything but hug Alice back. The sweet moment had been over far too soon, but Darla had been thinking about it the rest of the day. Sometimes she wondered if she was getting through to the kids but moments like the one she had shared with Alice reminded her that she was on the right path and that her work in Whale Harbor was making a difference.

The interaction with Alice had done more than that, though. She had felt such love for Alice and her other students in that moment, and she had realized that, if Rick never wanted to have kids, it would be okay. She loved Rick, and he was enough for her. She could have "kids" through working with the children at school. It might not be the life she had pictured, but it was still beautiful, and she realized that it truly was enough for her.

Grabbing the remote, Darla turned on the TV and started flicking through Netflix, looking for something brainless and lighthearted to help her relax after her day of work. She had just settled on some trashy reality TV when she heard keys jingling in the front door, which meant Rick was home. She flipped off the TV and sat up just as Rick came in the front door, looking as ruggedly handsome as ever. As always, her heart skipped a beat when she saw him and she jumped up to throw her arms around him.

"How's that for a warm welcome?" Rick asked, still keeping his arms around her and bending his head down to kiss her thoroughly. "Makes me want to go back out and come in again just so we can do this all over again!"

"Oh, stop." Darla laughed, swatting at him. "How was your day, hon?"

"It was fine. Better now that I'm back with you."

"Did the tours go well today?"

"They went okay. We only had one whale sighting, but at least there was one."

"That's too bad," Darla said sympathetically. "Well, you're home now."

"Not for long," Rick said, smiling down at her.

"What do you mean? Are you going somewhere?"

"*We're* going somewhere," Rick replied, his eyes alight with excitement. "I'm taking you out on a date!"

Darla's heart skipped another beat at the way he was looking at her and she knew she was smiling like a schoolgirl, but she couldn't help it. "Do I need to change into something else?"

"No, what you have on is perfect. What you do need to do is grab your art supplies and a canvas."

"Oohh, are we going painting together?"

"You already know it! The surprise is that I'm taking you to a place you haven't been before."

Darla scoffed at that. "I grew up in Whale Harbor—I'm pretty sure I know every inch of this place."

"Just you wait," Rick promised. "I'm pretty sure you haven't been where I'm taking you."

"I'll be the judge of that," she teased.

"Just grab your things," he growled, tickling her.

She squealed and twisted away from him, hurrying down the hallway to their bedroom and began gathering her painting supplies. Rick followed her, grabbing his painting supplies as well. A few minutes later they were loaded into the car and the two of them were on the road. Rick turned on the radio and then rested his hand on her knee, singing along with the radio as he drove. Darla joined in, rolling down the window and letting the wind tousle her curls. It was a perfect moment and she savored every second of it.

"So, any hints as to where you're taking me?" she asked after a moment.

Rick glanced at her, a roguish smile on his lips. "Come on, that would spoil the fun."

"Not even a teeny tiny hint?"

"Not even one," he said. "You'll see it soon enough."

Rick guided the car through the twisting roads that led away from Whale Harbor and further up the coast. They climbed higher and higher into the hills, heading toward the ocean. After about twenty minutes he parked the car.

"We have to walk from here," he said, coming around the car to open the door for Darla.

Darla took his proffered hand and climbed out of the car, breathing deeply of the salty air and savoring the feel of the ocean breeze against her face. It made her feel keenly alive, and she loved it. They went around to the trunk and pulled out their art supplies, then began walking down the dirt path. A few minutes later the trees cleared and they were standing on a cliff overlooking a stunning vista. In one direction, the ocean stretched as far as the eye could see, but if she turned, she could see the harbor and her small town spread out beneath her.

"Rick," she breathed, stunned at the mind-bending beauty in front of her. "This is..." She couldn't find the words.

"I know," he said softly, reaching for her hand. "It's beautiful, isn't it?"

"It's more than beautiful."

"I love this place," Rick said, staring out at the ocean with contented eyes. "This is a place I come to sometimes when I need to think. I thought you might like it."

"I can't believe I've never been here before."

"Not many people know about it. I stumbled across it kind of by accident, but I'm glad I did."

"Me too," Darla agreed fervently. "It's so inspiring up here! I can't wait to get painting."

They set up their easels, placing the canvases on them and opened up their painting supplies. Darla set hers up so that she was facing Whale Harbor, looking out over the small grid of her town, looking for all the places she knew and watching the boats in the harbor that stood out as brightly colored spots. This was a new view of her beloved hometown, and she couldn't wait to paint it from this perspective.

They both got to work, painting in companionable silence for a time, both inspired by the setting. As Darla worked, a fresh wave of love for Rick swelled in her heart and she glanced over at him. His brow was furrowed in concentration as he stared out at the ocean, his paintbrush held in his large, strong hand. She was always amazed at the delicate work those strong fingers could produce in his artwork.

How she loved this man beside her! He was everything to her, everything she didn't even know she was searching for. Who would have thought that she would find the love of her life not in the enormity of New York City, but in her tiny hometown of Whale Harbor? Rick caught her looking at him and he smiled at her softly, staring into her eyes in a way that made her heart beat faster. She had never felt so at ease with someone, so connected with another human being as she did with him.

Darla continued painting, the piece coming together beneath her paintbrush and, as she worked, her thoughts drifted again to the issue of whether or not they were going to have children. She should tell Rick about the epiphany she'd had earlier that day. She should tell him that she didn't need to have kids to be happy. He deserved to know, and she didn't want him to be in any doubt of how she felt about him.

She turned around to speak to him, just as he turned to her.

"Rick, I don't need to have kids," she blurted out, at exactly the same moment he said, "I'm willing to have children if you still want them."

They both stopped, blinking, and staring at each other in stunned surprise.

"What?" they both said at the same time, then laughed a little.

"Seriously, what did you just say?" Darla asked. "I'm not sure I heard you correctly."

Rick took a deep breath. "I was saying that I've thought through it a lot, and I'm willing to have kids if you still want them."

"But... I don't want you to compromise. I know you said you never pictured yourself having kids."

Rick nodded. "That's true. I had never *pictured* myself having kids, but that doesn't mean I'm not willing to have them. In fact, I'm more than willing, as long as they're yours and mine. I *want* to have children with you."

Darla couldn't believe her ears. She was reeling at the words Rick had just spoken, words she thought she would never hear from him.

"And you said you'd be willing to not have kids?" Rick asked, looking just as surprised as she felt.

"Yes," Darla replied. "I realized that all I need is you. I can still be fulfilled without having my own kids, especially because I kind of view my students as my own kiddos."

"You'd give that up for me?"

Darla nodded. "I would do anything for you."

Rick swallowed, his eyes suddenly liquid with unshed tears. "Hearing you say that means everything to me, but it doesn't change what I said. I want to have children with you. I want to build a family with you. You're my person, Darla." He paused, swallowing again. "The more I thought about it, the more I thought about our future together, I saw that it should include our children. And the more I thought about it, the more I loved the idea of it. I *want* to have children with you."

Darla lifted a trembling hand to her mouth, now blinking back tears herself. "You have no idea what this means to me..."

Rick came to her then, putting his arms around her and pulling her close. Darla rested her forehead against his chest, feeling his strong heartbeat against her face. The steady thump of it reassured her. She tilted her head back, and looked up into his eyes, laughing and crying at the same time as he lowered his head to hers and kissed her long and slow. She wrapped her arms around him and kissed him back fervently.

"Oh, my love," she whispered, when they finally broke apart and she had caught her breath. "I didn't think we'd ever work through this problem, but look at what our love did."

"I would do anything for you," Rick said simply.

"I know you would," she said, her voice thick with happy tears.

"Hey," he said softly, brushing away a tear that had slid from her eye. "Don't cry. This is a happy occasion!"

"These are happy tears," she explained, giving him a huge smile. "I've never been so happy in my life."

"And this is just the beginning," Rick promised. He studied her face, smiling like a kid. "And with such a stunning mom, our kids are going to be the most beautiful children in the world!"

Darla threw her head back and laughed. "I don't know about that."

"I do," Rick said seriously. "Our kids are going to be amazing, because they have you."

"And you."

Darla tightened her arms around Rick, resting her head against his chest once more and feeling the breeze curl around them. Earlier, she had thought the day was perfect, but that had been nothing compared to what she was feeling now.

"I love you, Rick Maroney," she murmured softly.

"And I love you, Darla Sims."

CHAPTER FIFTEEN

"Hey, man, good to see you," Wyatt called.

Trent, one of the guys he saw often at racing events, looked over at him and grinned. "Good to see you too, Jameson. Ready for me to kick your trash out on the course?"

"You'll be too busy eating my dust," Wyatt shot back, chuckling.

"Whatever you say, man," Trent said, shaking his head, then continued checking his quad before the race began.

Wyatt did the same, going over every inch of it to make sure that all was well. The day of the race had finally arrived and he was very much looking forward to competing. In the past, races used to hold a special significance for him as he saw them as a chance to prove something—plus the extreme adrenaline rush had been addictive for him. Racing had been an escape from mundane life and felt like taking things to the next level.

Racing wasn't like that for him anymore, though. He still loved it, but now he just saw it as a fun hobby. He had learned the hard way through his failed marriage what his hobby could do when he made it the entire focus of his life, and he wasn't planning to ever let racing take over his life the way it had before. Never again, especially now that he had set his sights on Marty Sims.

Speaking of Marty, he looked up from his quad and looked around the crowd, craning his neck to catch sight of her. She had said she would come and Marty was a woman of her word. He looked through the throngs of people but he didn't see her wavy brown hair anywhere. Disappointment pooled in his belly but he pushed it away, reminding himself that she would show up, it was just a matter of time.

"Nice quad, Jameson," Trent said, coming over to talk to him. "Not as good as mine, obviously, but still good looking."

"Thanks, man," Wyatt responded, ignoring the gibe against his quad. "I restored this bad boy myself."

"Nice!" The two fist bumped. "How fast can she go?"

Wyatt folded his arms and quirked up an eyebrow. "Faster than yours, if that's what you're wondering."

Trent hooted with laughter. "Come on, man, get real."

"I am. I've kicked your butt in races before. Don't think I won't do it again."

"Low blow, man. Low blow. And I've kicked your butt before too, don't forget."

"I don't seem to recall those times," Wyatt said, pretending to think hard. "You must be remembering it wrong."

"Whatever, dude. I'll prove it to you today out on the course."

"Bring it on. Loser buys drinks after."

"You're on," Trent said, reaching out to shake hands with Wyatt.

The announcer got on the microphone then, calling all the competitors to line up. Wyatt climbed onto his quad, driving it into position and feeling the pulse of adrenaline coursing through him. It was almost time. He looked out into the crowd again and, this time, he caught sight of Marty standing at the edge of the crowd looking nervous and out of place—

and more beautiful than ever. He lifted a hand and waved to her, and she cautiously raised a hand in return. His excitement kicked up several notches at the sight of her and he suddenly had the desire not just to beat Trent because of their bet but because he wanted to show off for Marty. Juvenile, he knew, but the desire was still there.

"On your mark," the announcer called, and Wyatt tensed. "Get set... Go!"

Wyatt revved and took off, the air filled with sandy dust from the dunes as the racers took off on the course. Wyatt pulled ahead early on, Trent right on his tail as he revved through the sandy course, flying over the top of a dune. Exhilaration hummed through his bones as he sailed through the course, taking a sharp right turn and cresting another dune. Trent pulled out ahead of him unexpectedly and Wyatt gritted his teeth, leaning forward on his quad and gunning it.

For the next few minutes they were neck and neck, one pulling ahead, then the other. Finally, Wyatt spotted the finish line up ahead and he kept his eyes trained on it, though he could feel Trent's presence. Wyatt hit the gas even harder, bursting ahead at the very last moment and sailing across the finish line milliseconds ahead of Trent. He hit the brake, coasting to a stop and feeling his heart pounding in his throat as the crowd screamed and cheered.

Pulling off his helmet, Wyatt felt a rush of pleasure and adrenaline as he pumped his fist in the air, the dust settling around him and the other racers. Trent hopped off his quad and came over to him, shaking his head but grinning nonetheless.

"That was a close thing, man!" Trent called.

"I thought you had me beat for a second there," Wyatt admitted.

"I did—I let you win, dude," Trent joked. "I knew you needed the ego boost."

Wyatt roared with laughter at that one and slapped Trent's shoulder jovially, then turned to wave at the crowd that was still whooping and cheering for him. The announcer came over and shook his hand, then lifted his hand in the air to show that he was the winner.

"Great race, dude," one of the other racers called, coming over to him to shake his hand. "You deserved the win with that kind of driving."

"Thanks, man," Wyatt responded.

The other racers came up one by one, shaking his hand and slapping him on the back. They were a good group of guys and he had raced with most of them many times before. It was a long time before he could make his way through the crowd of racers and well-wishers from the crowd and make his way to Marty's side. She was still standing on the outskirts of the crowd, looking out of place in the sea of racing fans.

"Marty!" he called as he approached her. "You came!"

Marty blinked, looking overwhelmed, but managed a small smile. "Of course! I promised I would, didn't I?"

"You did," he acknowledged, smiling down at her, still feeling the exultation and adrenaline from the race coursing through him. Marty was looking extra beautiful that day, he decided, and he wasn't sure if it was from the good feelings of the race or if she was just becoming more and more beautiful to him.

"Congratulations on your win," Marty said, her voice so soft he had to lean his ear down to her to hear her. "That was really amazing."

"Thanks," Wyatt said, smiling even more broadly. He was proud of the fact that he had won at a race his Marty was attending. "It was neck and neck there for a while. Almost lost to my buddy Trent."

"It was definitely close," Marty acknowledged.

There was a beat of awkward silence between them, and Wyatt finally noticed that she seemed stiff and tense. His smile faltered a little as the adrenaline began to fade away. Marty's hands were twisted together, her knuckles white, he noticed, and her eyes looked overwhelmed and distant.

"Hey, some of us were going to go grab some barbecue," Wyatt said, hoping to break the tension. "Want to come? Trent owes me a drink," he added, hoping to tease a smile out of her.

"Thanks, but I should get home," she said, taking a step back. She gave him a small smile. "Congratulations again. You did a great job," she said, her voice wooden.

Before he could say anything else, Marty turned and plunged through the crowd, heading toward the parking lot. He stood there, mouth open, watching her walk away and utter confusion took over. Had he done something wrong? Why had she booked it out of there so fast? And why had things been weird and tense between them? When she had come over to give him ideas for decorating his house they had talked together so easily, so naturally. He stared at her receding form, watching her wavy hair bounce as she walked and shook his head slowly. Something wasn't right.

"Hey, man, time to get you that drink I owe you," Trent said, coming up to him.

Wyatt wrenched his eyes away from where he had last seen Marty. "Sounds good, dude," he replied, hoping he sounded normal and happy. "Let's do it."

The two headed off to join the other racers who were making plans to grab some barbecue and drinks. As they slapped his back and congratulated him again, Wyatt tried to lose himself in the fun of the moment and call back the feelings of exhilaration he'd experienced in the race, but it was no use. He put on a good face for his friends, but the truth was that he wished Marty had stayed. He wished she was here with him.

And most of all, he wished he knew why she had run away like that.

CHAPTER SIXTEEN

The calico cat trotted beside Marty as she walked down the cobblestone street of downtown Whale Harbor, the leash held loosely in her hand. With her other hand, she took a sip of her latte from Seastar Espresso, trying—and failing—to enjoy the moment.

It was a calm Sunday afternoon, complete with a blue, cloudless sky overhead and a cool salty breeze from the ocean. It should have been perfect and, after the hectic Saturday she'd had at the Clownfish Eatery, Marty knew she should be in heaven enjoying her day off.

But she wasn't.

She still felt the residual stress from the chaotic shift at the diner and, if she was being honest with herself, she was still feeling off from her time at

Wyatt's quad race. Marty shuddered a little as she remembered the event. She had felt so out of place in the crowd of cheering, hardcore fans. If someone had pointed a spotlight on her and written "Misfit" on her forehead in Sharpie, she couldn't have felt more like she stuck out like a sore thumb.

It had been nice of Wyatt to include her, she knew that. And she also knew that he hadn't expected her to fall in love with the sport or be super knowledgeable about it or anything. Still, it had felt like one more reminder that she didn't really fit in with his interests or his lifestyle. It was a glaring reminder of just how different the two of them were, perhaps *too* different to ever make something work.

Marty shifted restlessly as she walked down the street, guiding the calico cat beside her. She just felt so... she didn't even know how to put into words what she was feeling. Restless? Sad? Uncertain?

Whatever's going on with me, I don't like it, she thought, taking another sip of her latte and once again failing to enjoy the warm drink.

She had felt off ever since the quad event and she was, quite frankly, tired of feeling like she was crawling out of her skin with the discomfort of it all. She kept telling herself to buck up and cheer up, but the mental pep talks weren't working. Instead, the cloud of conflicting emotions just seemed to weigh on her more heavily, making her thoughts spin and causing her to feel out of sorts with herself and everybody else.

Her eyes burned with fresh tears as she settled herself down on a public bench. The calico cat hopped up beside her and she stroked its fur absentmindedly, not even feeling better when she felt it purr at her touch. To her deep annoyance, a tear spilled over the edge of her lashes and trailed down her cheek, leaving a salty track. She swiped at it almost angrily, but it was soon followed by more tears.

Marty was, in a word, miserable.

What am I going to do about Wyatt? she thought, tracing a finger around the edge of her paper coffee cup. *This is such a mess.*

There was a huge part of her that wanted to take a chance on him, to just throw herself into her obvious attraction to him and see where it might lead. That part, however, was overshadowed by the cautious part of her. And that cautious part was screaming that they didn't stand a chance, that they were just too different to ever make things work. The little voice in her head that wouldn't let her sleep at night told her over and over again that going after

Wyatt would be a huge mistake, that it would only end in tears and misery.

Of course, she thought, *I'm already in tears and miserable, so what could it hurt to tell Wyatt how I feel?*

Instantly, the little voice in her head fought back, insisting that if she thought she felt terrible now, it was nothing compared to how she would feel if they did try to make a go of things. Marty swiped at another round of tears spilling down her cheeks, feeling overwhelmed by her emotions and torn about what to do about Wyatt.

"Marty?"

Marty jumped a little, looking up to see Wyatt rolling up on a quad beside her. She felt a hot flush burn through her cheeks, and she looked away, hoping that he hadn't seen the tears on her face. The quad's engine was super loud, but he turned off the ignition and quiet settled over them. She could feel his eyes raking over her face, even though she wasn't looking at him.

"Are you okay? What's wrong?"

"I'm fine," she responded, her voice muffled as she quickly swiped at her tears again. "Nothing's wrong."

There was a long pause and she didn't dare to look up at him.

"Do you mind if I sit down?" he finally asked.

Marty shrugged, scooting over to make room for him on the bench. In truth, the last thing she wanted right now was for Wyatt, of all people, to have appeared, but she couldn't change it now. Besides, there was still that tiny part of her that leapt at the sight of him, even in these awkward circumstances.

"Do you want to talk about it?" he asked after another long moment.

Marty shook her head and then, to her deep mortification, she burst into tears again. Using the sleeve of her long-sleeve t-shirt, she dabbed at her eyes, looking away from him and trying to get her crying under control. A moment later, she felt Wyatt's arm go around her, pulling her closer to his side and simply holding her while she cried. She leaned away, but he held firm and she gradually relaxed against his side.

"I'm sorry," she finally murmured when she could speak, though her voice was still thick with tears.

"Hey, there's no need to apologize," Wyatt responded, his voice kind. He rubbed his thumb up and down against her shoulder in a soothing gesture. "What's going on, Mar?"

Marty pulled in a slow, shuddering breath and shrugged. "It's just been a busy week. I must be more tired than I thought."

Wyatt speared her with a look. "Come on, I can tell it's more than that."

Marty's lip began to tremble again and she bit it to make it stop, petting her calico cat to give her hands something to do. Wyatt sat quietly beside her, his arm still around her, content to let her take her time. When she didn't speak, he finally ventured another question.

"I'm going to feel really stupid if I'm wrong, but... I can tell there's something more going on. Does it... does it have anything to do with me?"

Marty bit her lip harder. This was the moment of truth. She could fob him off with another lie and hope he believed it, or she could gather her courage and tell him what was really going on in her heart and mind. She took in a deep breath, held it, and then let it go, her mind racing. This was the moment. Could she be brave? Something within her snapped, and she finally turned to look at him, knowing what she was going to do.

"Yes," she whispered. "Yes, it has something to do with you."

She held her breath, waiting for him to respond. His eyes widened a little, but he nodded slowly.

"I thought it might," he murmured.

"Wyatt, I..." she paused, gulping, shocked with herself at what she was about to say. "I know this probably isn't going to come as a surprise, but... I have feelings for you."

"And that's so horrible that it's made you cry?" he teased gently, giving her a small smile, but his eyes looked tight and worried.

Marty shook her head. "No! It's not that."

"Then what is it?"

"It's just... we're so different, you know? I just don't see how we could ever make something work between us, and the quad race really solidified that for me. And I'm miserable, because... because I really, really like you."

To her surprise, the tightness left Wyatt's eyes and a genuine smile bloomed on his face.

"What?" she asked, swiping angrily at her tears.

"Nothing, it's just... it's nice to hear you say that you want me, because... I want you too."

Marty gasped, lifting a trembling hand to cover her mouth.

"Don't look so shocked," he teased, gently taking her hand away from her mouth and holding it with his free hand. "I don't think I've been that subtle."

"Well, I mean... I..." Marty stopped in confusion, feeling her cheeks flame up again.

Wyatt chuckled. "Man, it's taken us a long time to admit we have feelings for each other, hasn't it? We've only been friends our whole lives."

That sentence brought Marty crashing back to earth. "And what if we ruin our friendship by trying to make it something more? I meant what I said. I have no idea how we can make something work between us. We're just too different!"

Wyatt stopped smiling, his eyes becoming more intense as he gazed into hers. "I hear you, and I know you're scared. You have every right to be. I haven't been the most dependable person in the past. But, Marty, I've changed. Racing is no longer my life. I've found a balance that's much healthier now, and I've put down roots here in Whale Harbor. I meant what I told you before. I'm here to stay. I'm not going anywhere."

He paused, taking in a deep breath. "I know how important reliability is to you, and I'm doing my best to show you that I am the kind of man that you can rely on. I hope... I hope that you feel like you can take a chance on me, because I plan to do everything in my power to show you that you can trust me."

Marty sat, stunned, unable to speak. She searched his eyes, seeing the sincerity shining out from them. He meant every word he'd said, and that knowledge filled her with something that felt almost like hope.

"Oh, Marty," he whispered, running his thumb across her jaw and then sliding his hand to cup the back of her neck. He lowered his forehead to hers, resting against her and closing his eyes, just basking in her presence.

Marty's eyes fluttered closed, too, and they sat that way for a long minute. She could barely breathe at his closeness, but she found his presence comforting too. A moment later, he shifted and, before she knew what was happening, his lips brushed against hers. His kiss was feather-light, hesitant—a question. He lingered there, waiting to see what she would do. Before she could second-guess herself, Marty closed the gap between them and kissed him back, pouring all of her confusion and fear and love into the kiss. Her heart pounded wildly in her chest.

When they finally broke apart, Wyatt was staring at her, eyes wide.

"Wow," he murmured. "If I knew it would be like that, I would have kissed you a long time ago."

Marty laughed in spite of herself, knowing that her cheeks must be pinker than ever. She buried her face against his chest and felt his arms tighten around her.

"So," he said into her hair, "you really didn't like the quad race, did you?"

Marty sat up and looked at him, shaking her head as she chuckled sheepishly. "I actually thought it was really cool. I just felt *so* out of place, you know? I didn't know anything about the sport, and I guess I just felt stupid."

"Hmm..." Wyatt thought for a moment. "What if I taught you how to ride a quad? Then you would learn more about the sport and you might enjoy watching it more. Would you like that?"

To her surprise, the question filled her with excitement. She had never been the type to ride a quad, but it actually sounded really fun with Wyatt as her teacher. "Okay," she said. "Yeah, I think I'd like that."

Wyatt beamed at her. "That's my girl."

Just hearing him say that made her blush and butterflies erupted in her stomach. To cover her embarrassment, she picked up the calico cat and snuggled her close. Wyatt reached out and petted the cat, scratching between her ears.

"Does this little girl have a name yet?"

Marty shook her head. "Any ideas?"

"Hmm... how about Trouble? Since that's all I've been for you," he joked.

Marty laughed aloud. "Trouble... I like it. Trouble, do you like your new name?"

Trouble looked up at her and meowed.

"I'll take that as a yes," she said, smiling up at Wyatt. "By the way, I have some things I got for your house. I can bring them by tomorrow, if that works."

"Sounds good to me. Any excuse to see you," he said, kissing the tip of her nose, then he stood up. "I hate to go, but I was in the middle of transporting this quad to a customer's house. I'll see you tomorrow?"

Marty nodded, blowing him a kiss. "See you tomorrow."

Wyatt hopped back on the quad and revved it up, waving to her before cruising out of sight. As she watched him go, emotions swirled through Marty. The last few minutes had been a whirlwind—what with admitting they had feelings for each other and kissing for the first time, plus talking about everything she had been feeling before. Marty shook her head, overwhelmed by everything, but also glowing from the new direction things had taken. She looked down at her cat.

"You know what, Trouble? I think this calls for some ice cream."

CHAPTER SEVENTEEN

Wyatt's heart jumped a little in his chest as he heard the doorbell ring. That would be Marty, right on time as usual. They had planned that she would come over to work on his home decor a bit. In truth, Wyatt had never been one for interior design—he had always thought it was somewhat frivolous. But working with Marty was changing his mind in ways he had never expected. Watching her work inspired him and he was coming to realize that, not only was she talented, but that her work made a space entirely transform into something that actually felt like a real home.

Wyatt pulled the door open and his heart thudded as Marty's honey brown eyes looked up into his. "Hey," he said softly, leaning against the door frame and hoping he looked casual.

Marty held up two sample cans of paint. "I come bearing gifts."

"Paint for the living room?"

"Yes, sir," she teased. "Are you going to let me in so I can show you what I've picked out?"

Wyatt felt his cheeks heating up at that, but he just smiled and stepped back so she could enter. As she walked past he caught a whiff of her citrusy perfume and he silently breathed deeply of it.

"So, what colors did you pick out?"

"Patience, patience," Marty teased, already unscrewing the lids of the paint and pulling out two paintbrushes. "I'm going to paint a swatch of each on the wall and we can see which one you like best."

While he watched, Marty painted a large square of his wall to a sandy beige color, then picked up the other paintbrush and painted a swatch of wall a light gray, although he noticed that the gray had blue undertones. He studied them, tilting his head to the side and taking both of them in.

"They both coordinate well with the brown leather sofa you picked out," Marty said, screwing the lids back onto the paint cans and walking over to the sink to wash the brushes.

Wyatt walked around the room, looking at the colors from different vantage points to see how it changed based on the lighting. A moment later, clean brushes in hand, Marty joined him.

"Which way are you leaning?" she asked. "Or, if you don't like either color, I can get more samples."

"No, I like both of these. That's kind of the problem. What are your thoughts?"

"Well," Marty said slowly, studying them both. "I'm leaning toward the sand color—it warms up the room and makes it feel cozier, plus it would look great with some of the wall decor I have in mind."

"Can I see?"

"Sure, let me get my iPad." Marty dug in her bag and pulled out her iPad, pulling up some pictures. "There's this funky metal wall decor that I think shows the more mechanically-minded parts of you, and it would really pop against the sand color for the wall."

Wyatt looked closer at the iPad, his eyes widening. "I love it!"

"I thought you might," Marty said with a grin. "And then, of course, there's this ocean view piece that Darla's been working on."

Wyatt felt his mouth drop open. "She would give me one of her pieces?"

"Yes. I told her what I was looking for and she started working on it right away."

"A Darla Sims original in a room decorated by Marty Sims... I'm going to be the talk of the town," he joked.

Marty rolled her eyes, but she looked pleased.

"Do you have any pictures of Darla's piece?"

Marty shook her head. "Not yet, but the blues and greens in it would look stunning against the sand color."

Wyatt lifted his hands, laughing. "All right, all right, I think I'm sold. I love the sandy color, so I'm not opposed to it." He leaned against the wall, looking down at Marty. "You know, I always knew you were going to be successful in your interior design business."

"You did?"

"Yup. Not only are you insanely talented, but you're reliable and steady." He looked down at his hands, suddenly all too aware of the qualities that he lacked. "Something that isn't my forte," he admitted.

"But you're working on it," Marty said softly. "And that counts for something. Plus, you have an adventurous spirit I've always been jealous of. I mean, look at all your medals from quad and dirt bike racing," she said, waving to the shelf that held his various medals and trophies.

Wyatt followed her gaze and looked at his medals and trophies too. "There was a time where that was my whole life," he said softly.

"But not any more?"

Wyatt shook his head seriously. "No. Not anymore. I mean, don't get me wrong, I still love racing, but I've learned not to let a hobby become more important than what really matters, what's really supposed to last. Never again."

There was a long, pregnant pause that stretched between them. Wyatt knew they were both thinking about his divorce from Helen and probably also about how flaky he had been in the past with Marty, swooping in and out of her life with no notice. The thought made him cringe, but he saw no judgment in Marty's eyes when he finally dared to look at her. Instead, she was looking at him with such compassion that it made his heart melt and he suddenly had the urge to pull her into his arms and kiss her.

Gathering his courage, he stuffed his hands into his pockets and finally asked the question that had been on his mind all day. "So... how do you feel about what happened yesterday?"

Marty raised an eyebrow, but her cheeks were suddenly rosy. "You mean the kiss?"

"Yeah, that," Wyatt replied, unable to keep from laughing a little. "I know it was probably... unexpected."

"I mean, we've never been anything but friends, and we've been friends our whole lives."

"I think that there was more going on but that we just never acknowledged. A spark we just kind of... ignored."

Marty's cheeks were absolutely flaming. "I'll be honest—I always had a crush on you, but I was way too afraid to act on it."

"Why didn't you say something sooner?"

Marty laughed and ran a hand through her wavy hair. "Like I said, I was way too afraid to act on it." She gulped, looking him in the eye. "To be honest, I'm not a risk taker, so I'm still scared right now," she admitted, her voice soft and vulnerable.

Wyatt reached out and took her hand, lacing his fingers through hers. "Honestly, I'm scared too."

Marty blinked, then smiled a little. "Really?"

"Really. It feels like a big leap, but it's a leap I want to take. With you. I really like you, and being back in Whale Harbor and spending time with you has really solidified that for me."

"I really like you too," Marty whispered, squeezing his hand.

Wyatt felt his heart thumping hard in his chest. "The good news is that we don't have to know exactly what this is, right this second. We don't have to put a label on it or have a timeline. We can just let things unfold and develop the way that they will."

Marty breathed a sigh of relief. "So we're taking it slow. I like that."

Wyatt leaned forward and kissed her on the forehead. "As slow as you want to take things. You set the speed and I'll follow."

Tentatively, Marty stepped into his arms and gave him a hug. It was simple and sweet, and it filled his heart right up to the brim. Now that they'd had this conversation and gotten everything out into the open, Wyatt felt a lot more at peace, a lot more able to relax.

"So," he said, stepping back but still keeping a hold of her hand. "I think we've picked out my paint color."

"Excellent! And you like the wall decor I've chosen?"

"I love it," he assured her, and he meant it. She had picked out pieces he never would have thought of but that he loved.

"And you're going to help with the painting, right?" she asked, poking him in the ribs.

"Me?" he asked, pretending to look shocked. "I thought that was all you!"

Marty poked him again and he laughed, pulling her into his arms. "Just kidding, just kidding. Of course I'm going to help you with the painting."

In truth, he was looking forward to it. Besides the fact that it would make his home look better, it meant spending more time with Marty, something he desperately wanted.

"Oh," he said, remembering something else. "Are you still good to go to the dunes with me tomorrow after work?"

Marty nodded, but she bit her lip, looking a little afraid. "I'm still good to go."

Wyatt laughed, smoothing out the crease between her eyes with his thumb. "Don't look so nervous! It's going to be a lot of fun and, just like we're doing with our relationship, we'll take things slow."

Marty smiled, looking relieved. "Okay, then. That sounds good."

"You're going to have a great time," he promised. "I can't wait to show you the world of quad riding!"

CHAPTER EIGHTEEN

Marty pushed the vacuum back and forth across her living room carpet half-heartedly. She glanced at the clock on her wall, which read 4:45. She needed to leave to meet Wyatt soon, but she'd been putting it off all day for some reason.

He was taking her to the dunes to teach her how to ride a quad and she had spent the whole day dillydallying. She'd taken Trouble for a walk, she'd deep cleaned her kitchen, shredded old tax documents, and now she was vacuuming her living room carpet—-which she had just vacuumed the previous day and didn't need to be done again yet.

When she thought about seeing Wyatt again, butterflies erupted in her stomach. And learning how to ride a quad? She was... excited, she supposed, although that wasn't fully true. She was also deathly terrified. Quad riding was way outside of her comfort zone—it was unlike anything she'd ever done before. The speed, the danger, the adrenaline... all of those things made it a distinctly unusual activity for her.

She glanced at the clock again and saw that the minute hands had inched nearer to five. She needed to leave now if she was going to be at Wyatt's on time, and she did pride herself on her punctuality. Nerves thrumming through her, she turned off the vacuum and grabbed her purse, locking the front door behind her and climbing into her car. Just as she was about to put her keys in the ignition, her cell phone rang.

She fished it out of her bag and saw that Rick was calling. Starting up the car, she answered the call.

"Hey, Rick, what's up?"

"Hey, Marty, how are you?"

"I'm actually on my way to a meeting." She didn't add that the "meeting" was a quad lesson with Wyatt.

"Okay, then, I'll keep this short." Rick pulled in a deep breath. "I need your help with something. Something big."

Marty only just held back a gasp. She knew in

her gut what this had to be about—-Rick needing her help with something big? He *had* to be proposing to her sister.

"Sure, what do you need help with?"

"I think we both know why I'm calling," Rick said, his voice filled with warmth and excitement. "I have big plans for the future with Darla, and I need your help to pull it off."

"Anything," Marty promised. "What can I do to help?"

"Okay, here's what I was thinking..."

For the rest of the drive, Rick filled Marty in on what her part would be in the surprise proposal for Darla. Excitement filled Marty as she listened and chimed in. All too soon, Rick was signing off of the call and Marty was pulling into Wyatt's driveway. After she said goodbye, Marty stared at Wyatt's house for a moment, trying to reorient herself in the present moment. She set aside thoughts about Darla's impending engagement and refocused on the upcoming quad lesson.

She took a deep breath, trying to calm the butterflies in her stomach, but it was no use. They insisted on taking flight and flapping their wings wildly. She felt a little nauseous, too, if she was being honest, but that dissipated the moment Wyatt opened his front door and grinned down at her. Then the butterflies were flapping for a far different reason. Wyatt was practically glowing with excitement. His gray eyes were bright and clear and his smile could have rivaled the sun in its brilliancy.

"Are you ready to go?" he asked. "I've packed us a picnic dinner to eat at the dunes."

Marty blinked, a touch surprised by that. She had thought this would just be a lesson, but the picnic dinner implied that this was a legitimate date. It was just one more reminder that Wyatt was really serious about her and that he really wanted to prove that he was ready for something lasting. Marty smiled up at him, pleased down to her toes with him.

"I... think I'm ready," she said, her nerves coming back.

"Hey, you're going to be great," he assured her, reaching out and squeezing her hand. "We're going to take it slow, remember? No need to be nervous."

"Right," Marty said with a firm nod, putting on a braver face than she felt inside.

"Come on. We'll take my truck. I've got the quad hooked on to the back."

By his truck, Wyatt held the door open for Marty and then headed around the truck and climbed into the driver's side. He revved up the truck and carefully backed out of the driveway, quad in tow.

"How's your day been?"

Marty couldn't help but smile at that. "Wildly productive, actually."

Wyatt quirked up an eyebrow at that. "Yeah? How come?"

"I was so nervous about this that I ended up doing a ton of cleaning at my house," she admitted with a chuckle.

"Oh, Mar..." Wyatt chuckled too. "Well, at least you got a clean house out of it." He shot a glance at Marty. "Not that your house needed it, I'll bet. You keep that place spic and span."

"Some of the cleaning may have been redundant," Marty admitted, thinking about vacuuming the living room carpet two days in a row.

"I'm really glad you showed up today, since you're so nervous," Wyatt said softly, reaching out one hand and taking hers in his.

Marty threaded her fingers through his. "I'm glad I came too," she said, surprised to find that she meant it.

Wyatt kept her mind occupied the rest of the drive with light, teasing conversation, and she had almost forgotten her nerves by the time they arrived at the dunes. Wyatt turned off the truck and climbed out to start unloading the quad. Marty got out of the truck more slowly, eyeing the dunes with distrust. They looked so big up close, and she was going to potentially drive a quad on them?

"Good news," Wyatt called to her from the back of the truck. "We got here in time to watch the sunset."

Marty looked up at the sky, noting that the sun was heading toward the horizon. The area really *was* beautiful. Even with her nerves she could appreciate that. The sky was already turning a light pink in places and she knew that the sunset was going to be spectacular. Even better, she was going to share that sunset with Wyatt.

"Okay, ready to climb up?" Wyatt asked.

Marty walked back to him to find him sitting on the quad, ready to go. She gulped, but climbed up in front of him, her heart thumping hard as she felt his chest against her back. His arms circled around her then and her heart beat even faster as he showed her the controls and how they worked. She mentally shook herself, telling herself to pay attention to what he was saying.

Wyatt went over all the controls, how to start and stop the quad, and steering. She appreciated that he went over everything, even the most basic details, but he didn't do it in a way that made her feel patronized. She gradually relaxed against him as he talked, listening intently and asking questions along the way.

"Okay, ready to take it for a spin?" he asked.

Marty gulped and then squared her shoulders, nodding. Now that she knew how the quad worked, she felt a bit more ready. "We'll just keep it on the flat part for now, right?"

"Of course. We won't go on the dunes until you're ready."

Marty nodded and started up the quad, feeling it rumble beneath her. Carefully, she pulled forward, Wyatt guiding her.

"Easy does it, you're doing great," he encouraged her.

With his guidance, Marty sped up a little, making some large figure eights. Wyatt whooped behind her, cheering her on, and Marty was surprised to find that she was actually enjoying herself. After practicing for about twenty minutes, Wyatt asked her if she wanted to take it up on the dunes and Marty gathered her courage.

"Let's do it!" she called.

Revving up the engine, she drove up the side of

the dune and then down the other, not getting any air but feeling the adrenaline rush of flying up and down the dune. She laughed aloud, wind in her face, as she drove. She drove down the side of the dune, back to the flat ground and turned off the engine.

"You were great!" Wyatt exclaimed, hugging her tightly.

"Thanks! It was way more fun than I was expecting."

"That's because you're a natural."

"I don't know about that," Marty said, but she was pleased nonetheless.

She climbed off the quad and he followed, looking at her in a way that made her heart race. Slowly, he stepped toward her and reached out a hand to cup her face. Not losing eye contact with her, he slowly lowered his head toward hers. Her eyes fluttered shut as he pressed his lips to hers and her heart felt like it might explode as the kiss deepened. Their first kiss was amazing, but this one was even better because this one was intentional, not just something that happened on the spur of the moment. She could tell Wyatt had been thinking about kissing her like this for a while. When they finally broke apart, Marty was breathless, but she was pleased to note that Wyatt was too.

"Do you want to take the quad out for a quick spin?" Marty asked the question more to cover her embarrassment, but she also knew he was probably dying to get some actual speed.

"Are you sure?"

"Absolutely!"

Wyatt grinned like a kid, hopping onto the quad and taking off. He zoomed up the dune, catching air as he sailed over the top. Watching that stunt made Marty's heart race, but more with nerves than anything else. He zoomed down the other side and then popped a wheelie, and Marty had to close her eyes for a moment with fear. Watching him, Marty could see his daredevil streak, could see what a kick he got out of the danger. He popped another wheelie, riding on the back two wheels for a few seconds and then spinning off into a different direction. It was all Marty could do to keep from shrieking aloud. After a few minutes, he returned to her side, pulling off his helmet, his sandy hair adorably mussed. Marty's heart rate was only just now returning to normal after watching him risk his neck, but she was glad that he had come back to her safely.

"That'll be you in no time," he said, his eyes bright with excitement from the ride.

"Um, I think I'd rather watch than do that," she said with a scared laugh.

"You say that now, but I know there's a daredevil in there somewhere," he teased.

"I wouldn't be too sure about that," Marty hedged. "I'm just little old me."

"I happen to like 'little old you'," Wyatt shot back.

Wyatt tossed aside his helmet and swept her up in his arms, spinning her around and then lowering his head to kiss her, clearly still caught up in the moment. Marty laughed against his lips, trying to let herself get caught up in the adventurousness of the moment, but if truth be told, she was a little scared too. It was easy to get enticed in his spirit when she was in his strong arms, but they were so different when it came down to it. As Wyatt kissed her, there was a part of her brain that stayed caught up in her worries. Thoughts circled in her head.

Could she ever keep up with him, with his energy and thirst for adventure? Could they ever find a middle ground between their two personalities? As Marty kissed him back, trying to shut out that little voice in her head, she had to admit that she wasn't so sure.

CHAPTER NINETEEN

Wyatt tossed his screwdriver onto his workbench and climbed to his feet, groaning a little as he stretched. It had been a busy morning of quad restoration and, if his grumbling stomach was any indication, it was time to eat.

He wiped off his hands on a rag and then pulled his phone from his pocket. As he had expected, it was almost noon.

Whistling, he walked to the front of his shop and flipped the sign on the door around so that it read 'Closed' and then headed out the door, locking it behind him.

Usually he packed a lunch or headed home, but today he was in the mood for lobster ravioli, and the best place to get that was, of course, the Clownfish

Eatery. Hands in his pockets, he strolled down the sidewalk toward the diner, enjoying the uncharacteristically warm fall day and breathing in the salty scent of the ocean breeze.

The fresh air and sunshine felt good after being cooped up in his workshop all morning, but he was pleased about the work he'd managed to get done that day. By the end of the day he should have the quad finished up and ready to sell, which pleased him greatly.

Sauntering up the steps to the restaurant, he pulled open the door of the Clownfish Eatery, breathing in the heady scents of delicious cooked food. Rose looked up from the hostess stand, her wrinkled face breaking into a smile at the sight of him.

"Wyatt! So good to see you, son," Rose said, coming out from behind the stand to give him a hug, her fluffy white hair tickling his chin as she did so. "Coming in for some lunch?"

"Yes, ma'am. I've had your lobster ravioli on my mind all morning!"

"You've come to the right place, then. Table for one?"

"Yup."

Rose speared him with a look. "And just when

are you going to come in here asking for a table for two? You're too good of a young man to be single, you know," she admonished him.

Wyatt grinned at her, leaning forward conspiratorially. "Actually, there may be some progress on that front."

"Oh? Do tell," Rose said, leading him to one of the benches that sat in the waiting area of the diner.

"Well, I took Marty out on a date this past week."

Rose gasped. "You did?"

Wyatt nodded.

"Well, it's about time!" Rose folded her arms and nodded firmly. "You're quite the lucky man, you know."

"Oh, I know it," Wyatt agreed fervently. "Marty is a woman in a million."

"That she is, and don't you ever forget it!"

"I promise you, I won't." Wyatt paused, frowning a little. "Truth be told, I'm still not sure she's fully convinced that I'm someone she could be with long-term. I think my past scares her a little."

"What do you mean?"

"Well, you know how steady and reliable Marty is."

"Oh, yes."

"Right. Well, I know she values stability, and in the past that hasn't exactly been my strong suit."

Rose nodded thoughtfully, then patted him on the knee. "Well, actions are everything. Marty is a sensible and careful young woman. Give her some time to see that you've changed and it will be worth it. You don't have to say anything to convince her, you just have to show her in little and big ways that she is what you want."

"She really is."

"Then make sure everything you do reminds her of that."

Wyatt smiled. "Thank you. You always have the best advice."

Rose winked at him, smiling up at him. "Well, when you've lived as long as I have, you gain a lot of life experience. It has to be good for something, doesn't it?"

"You're a wealth of good advice from all that life experience, ma'am," Wyatt said, winking at her.

She reached out and patted his cheek. "You're a good boy, and Marty is a good girl. You'd be a good match."

"You really think so?"

"I do," Rose said, nodding emphatically. "I've known both of you since you were in diapers. I have a good sense about these things. Now," she said, leaning toward him, "I'm not saying that it will be easy. Marty is a careful woman, and I think she's built up some defenses around herself."

"I think she has too," Wyatt agreed.

"That being said, she's worth the work you'll have to put in to overcome those defenses. The best ones always are."

"She's definitely worth the work and the wait. I'm going to do my best not to disrupt her life, but just be there and show her that I think she's incredible the way she is. I think sometimes she thinks she needs to change or be different, but I don't see it that way." Wyatt looked out the window, remembering the quad race. "You know, I took Marty to one of my quad races a while ago and I could tell she felt out of place. I could sense that she felt like she didn't fit in with the other folks at the race, and I wonder if she feels like she doesn't fit in with me either."

"It's quite possible," Rose said thoughtfully. "She may think the two of you are too different."

"I don't ever want her to feel that way with me. I want her to always know that there's room in my life for her, just as she is."

"That's a very mature way to look at things, son,"

Rose said softly. "And I know that Marty will be able to feel that from you as long as you take your time and just keep showing her that you love her as she is."

Wyatt nodded, thinking about Marty and how much he cared about her. She was such a special woman. He still couldn't believe it had taken him so long to see what had been right in front of him practically his whole life, but here he was. He just hoped she would give him a chance to show her just how much he cared for her.

"Do you have any fun plans lined up for her?" Rose was asking, pulling him from his thoughts.

"What? Oh, yes, actually. Marty is helping me to spruce up my house a little—make it less of a barren bachelor pad and all that—and she's actually coming over tonight to work on it with me."

"That's wonderful, son," Rose said, beaming at him, her blue eyes alight with approval. "I'm sure your house will look amazing when it's finished. She's so talented."

"Don't I know it," Wyatt agreed fervently. "She's working magic on my place. It's becoming quite homey."

"If it's anything like her shop, I'm sure it will look amazing."

"You'll have to come by and see it when it's all done."

Rose nodded and they sat in companionable silence for a moment, then Rose shifted and looked up at him, her eyes searching.

"And what about the October Showdown?" Rose asked, watching him closely. "Are you still competing in that or have you outgrown it?"

"Oh, I'm absolutely still competing," Wyatt said quickly. "In fact, I'm looking to win again this year if I can. That's the hope, at least."

"I see," Rose said quietly, then patted his knee and stood up. "Let's get you that table. I'm sure you're starving."

Wyatt blinked, a bit floored by the abrupt end to their conversation, but he stood up as well. Rose led him to a table by a window overlooking the harbor and then left to place his order for lobster ravioli in the kitchen. She returned a moment later with his drink and then left him to wait for his food. He squeezed a wedge of lemon into his water and took a sip, looking out at the harbor thoughtfully, not really seeing the boats bobbing in the water.

I gave Rose that answer about the quad race really fast, he realized after a moment.

He hadn't even hesitated when she'd asked about

the race. His response had been automatic, a knee-jerk reaction. That was a bit like the old Wyatt, but he knew that he truly had changed. Quad racing, which used to be an obsession of his, was now just a hobby. Something he did for fun but not something that defined his life. There was no need to make that adrenaline-seeking his entire life the way it once had been.

As he realized that, his thoughts drifted back to Marty, to her sweet and soft presence. He had missed out on having that as a constant in his life for too long, and he definitely wasn't going to lose her to thrill seeking the way he had lost his ex-wife. As for Marty, he was determined not to take her for granted again.

And maybe, he thought as his food came out and he took a bite, *maybe there's another kind of rush that's better than adrenaline—love.*

CHAPTER TWENTY

Marty hummed along with the radio as she drove toward Wyatt's house. He'd swung by the shop earlier that day to drop off a key, saying that he would be a little late—apparently a customer had come in needing same-day repairs for a competition. Marty didn't mind getting started alone. She liked to paint—there was something so soothing about the rolling motion and watching a space transform before her very eyes.

The breeze coming through her rolled-down car windows tousled her hair, but she didn't mind. She was going to see Wyatt that evening and she was feeling good. With one hand, she turned up the radio, singing along now with the music. A few minutes later, she arrived at his house and parked in his driveway, still humming to herself as she climbed out of the car and then grabbed the painting supplies.

Juggling the painting supplies into one arm, she fished in her pocket for the key Wyatt had given her and put it into the front door's lock, then hesitated. It felt like an invasion to just waltz right into his home, even though he had given her a key and given her instructions to do so.

He wanted you to get started on the painting, stop being a ninny about it, she told herself.

Pushing down the feeling that she was doing something she shouldn't, Marty turned the key in the lock and pushed open the front door. She closed the door behind her, breathing in the faint scent of Wyatt's cologne that still lingered in the air. The house was silent around her and she stood in the entryway for a moment, contemplating the living room before her and how it would look when it was all painted.

"Well, just standing around won't get the job done," she said aloud.

Setting the painting supplies down, she pulled her phone from her pocket and turned on some music, then got to work. First, she would need to lay down plastic sheeting over the carpet, using painters' tape to hold it down. She didn't want any paint to drip on the carpet and ruin it, but laying out the plastic and cutting it to size was a big job. Wyatt still hadn't fully unpacked, and there were a lot of unpacked boxes stacked in the living room. Humming along with the music, she began hefting the boxes out of the way, stacking them in the bedroom and the kitchen.

As she worked, she couldn't help but daydream about their evening at the dunes. She could still feel Wyatt's arms around her as he sat behind her on the quad, could feel the wind in her hair and hear the sound of Wyatt's laughter ringing through the air. She sighed dreamily, replaying their fantastic kiss. She loved how he was when they were together—there seemed to be a new mellowness about him that hadn't been there when they were growing up.

Or is that just wishful thinking? a little voice whispered in the back of her mind.

"Oh, hush," she grumbled aloud, scowling at nothing.

What she wouldn't give to just be able to daydream about Wyatt without doubts and fears getting in the way. Why couldn't she just fully let herself go and relax? Why couldn't she just relinquish control and see where things led the two of them?

To distract herself, Marty finished taping down the plastic sheeting and then grabbed the can of paint, prying it open and using the wooden stick that came with it to stir the paint until it was well mixed again. As she did so, she admired the color they had picked out. The sandy hue would look perfect on Wyatt's walls and it would really warm up the space and provide the perfect backdrop for the furnishings and decorations Marty had picked out.

Marty poured some paint into the painter's tray and prepared a roller brush. As she worked, she thought about the other plans she had for his house, including the artwork she had commissioned for his living room and the dining room table she had seen online that she thought Wyatt should order. It was masculine and sculptural, and it would look awesome in his kitchen.

Of course, if she were living there, it wouldn't be the table she would pick out for herself. She would have picked something more delicate and feminine. And, of course, those feminine touches would continue throughout the house, with more throw pillows on the couch and a deep plush rug in the bedroom to sink into when walking from the bed to the bathroom or closet.

"What am I thinking?" Marty said suddenly, breaking the quiet in the house.

She could feel a flush suffusing her cheeks. She couldn't believe she had been daydreaming about living with Wyatt. It was so premature—she still had so many doubts and they had only kissed twice. She gulped, fanning herself and entirely grateful that Wyatt wasn't around and couldn't read her thoughts.

Girl, you've got to pull it together, she warned herself. *Falling for Wyatt Jameson when he wasn't ready to settle down is what got you into trouble in the past. Don't go making the same mistake now.*

Her own internal warning ringing through her head, Marty was about to dip the roller brush into the paint tray when she realized there was still one more box she hadn't moved out of the way. She set the roller down and walked over to the box, picking it up. As she did so, she tripped on the plastic sheeting beneath her that had bunched up a little and the box tumbled from her arms, popping open. It fell to the floor, pictures and papers spilling from it.

Marty groaned and crouched down to begin clearing up the mess, then froze where she stood. The pictures were all of Wyatt and his ex-wife,

Helen. A sick feeling bubbled in her stomach as she bent down and got closer, picking up first one photo, then another, and studying them. In the first one, Wyatt had his arms around Helen, who had her head thrown back while she laughed. Wyatt was smiling down at her with an expression of tenderness and love.

Marty sank to the floor with a thud, clutching the photo and staring at it. She couldn't tear her eyes away from the image of the two of them. They looked so happy, so in love. Wyatt's adoration of Helen was almost palpable. The sick feeling in her stomach grew and Marty finally set the picture inside the box, turning it face down.

Why has Wyatt kept all of these? Does he still have feelings for Helen?

Marty felt a numbness begin to steal over her. Why in the world would Wyatt hold onto photos and keepsakes from his first marriage if it had ended? With shaking fingers, she picked up the next photo, which showed Helen kissing Wyatt's cheek while he smiled at the camera, his eyes bright and full of love. Photo after photo showed the two of them together— walking along the beach, standing at the front of a church on their wedding day, traveling for their honeymoon...

Trembling, Marty gathered the stack of pictures up and placed them into the box, her mind reeling as emotions poured over her. She tried to talk herself out of having a full-blown melt down, but it was difficult. Already, she couldn't help but compare herself to Wyatt's beautiful ex-wife.

Had Helen been more adventurous than she was? Did Wyatt miss that about his ex-wife? Was Marty just a rebound until he found the courage to go back to Helen or find someone better suited to himself? He said he liked her the way she was, but what if he got bored with her tame life and moved on, just the way he had from Helen? Marty shuddered, feeling bile rise in her throat.

Hastily, she cleaned up the rest of the photos and put the box in Wyatt's bedroom, closing the door after. She returned to the living room, feeling almost physically ill.

"Stop it," she said aloud to the empty room, rubbing her arms and shaking a little. "It doesn't necessarily mean anything!"

Just because Wyatt hadn't burned all the photos from his first marriage didn't mean that he still had feelings for Helen, Marty told herself. It wasn't a crime to treasure good memories, and she needed to stop reading into it.

Even though she was giving herself solid advice, Marty still felt sick to her stomach and she couldn't stop worrying about all the new feelings and questions that finding those photos had brought to the surface.

Just then, she heard the front door open and whirled around to find Wyatt stepping inside the entryway.

"Hey," he called. "Sorry I'm late."

"No worries," she said, her voice sounding choked and strangled even to her own ears. "I just got here a little bit ago, and I've barely even gotten started."

Wyatt didn't seem to hear the strange tone of her voice as he smiled and walked into the room. "Well, it looks like you've gotten things set up to paint, which is half the battle. Thanks for doing that!"

"No problem."

"You're a gem, you know that?" Wyatt asked, smiling down at her, his eyes gazing into hers.

The way he was looking at her made her stomach flip and flutter with sudden butterflies that warred with the conflicting emotions that finding the photographs had stirred up. Wyatt took a step closer, reaching out and tugging her closer to him, then bending down and kissing her. Marty hesitated beneath his kiss, then kissed him back quickly and stepped back, breaking the kiss off.

Wyatt's brow wrinkled as he looked down at her. "You okay? Are we good?"

Marty nodded, not wanting to tell him what she'd found and suddenly feeling like the room was too small. "Just anxious to get started," she said, forcing a cheer into her voice that she didn't feel. "Come on, these walls aren't going to paint themselves."

Wyatt chuckled, seeming to accept her explanation. "Remind me not to get in the way when you're in design mode."

"That's right, mister," she joked lamely, picking up her roller and dipping it into the paint.

Wyatt grabbed a roller as well and the two of them got to work. Marty picked a different wall than him so she could turn her back to him and she wouldn't have to school her expression into one of good humor. She threw herself into the painting, glad she had a task on which to focus her mind.

As she worked, still feeling a little nauseous, she could already tell it was going to be a long night.

CHAPTER TWENTY-ONE

"Great choice, man!" Wyatt said, reaching out to shake his customer's hand. "You're going to love this quad."

"I can already tell that I will," the man responded, grinning widely. "I can't wait to take this baby out on the dunes."

"She's a fast one, be ready."

"I live for speed, so that's just a plus in my book."

Wyatt laughed, slapping the man's shoulder jovially. "Let's get you rung up at the cash register and then we can work out delivery details."

The man followed Wyatt up to the front of the shop and pulled out his credit card, still talking about how excited he was to take the quad out for a spin. They got him taken care of, arranged delivery details, and then, with one last loving look at the quad, the man left the shop. Wyatt pumped his fist in the air after the man left. Business was going great and he couldn't be happier with how his shop was doing, especially since opening a small business of any kind was a risk. It looked like his hunch that Whale Harbor could use a quad/bike shop had been correct.

Whistling, he meandered to the back of the shop where he was currently restoring a dirt bike and picked up his screwdriver, ready to get to work in the lull between customers. Before he could get started, though, his cell phone began buzzing in his pocket. Setting the screwdriver down, he pulled his phone from his pocket and saw that his father was calling. He slid the green button to answer the call.

"Hey, Pops, what's up?"

"Hey, son, I've got big news for you," Frank said, his voice full of excitement.

Wyatt's curiosity was instantly piqued. "Yeah? What is it?"

"One of my employees, Richard—you remember Richard, right?"

"Yeah."

"Right, well, Richard has been talking about opening a shop in Newport, which would further expand our business."

Wyatt whistled. "Good for him!"

"That's all well and good, but I wasn't calling just to chat about it," Frank said, laughing, "I'm calling because Richard is going to need some help."

"Okay..."

"He wants to know if you'd like to be a partial owner in his shop too."

Wyatt's heart thudded with excitement. This was a really big deal. Being a partner in another shop meant more revenue, more opportunities to expand, reaching more clientele... Suddenly he froze on the spot, barely even breathing. It also meant being away from Whale Harbor more often and traveling for work all the time. His heart rate slowed and he closed his eyes, blowing out a slow breath.

"Son?"

"I'm here, Dad. Just thinking."

"I thought you'd be excited..."

"I am," Wyatt admitted, "but I think I'm going to have to pass."

There was a long pause. "You're going to pass on this opportunity? Why in the world would you do that? Do you realize what a big deal this is?"

Wyatt ran a hand through his hair, a little frustrated. "I do realize what a big deal it is."

"Look, son, why don't you take some time to think this over."

Wyatt shook his head. "No, I don't need time. My mind is made up."

There was another long pause. "What's going on, son? Why don't you want to do this?"

Wyatt sucked in a breath, hoping his father would understand. "Look, the truth is that I can't do it because I want to pursue Marty. I'm really interested in her, Dad."

"Marty, huh?"

"Yes." The word hung between them. "I've found the thing that makes me happy, and it's her. I just can't be leaving town all the time—I need to show her that I'm here to stay, that I'm not always going to be flying around all the time."

"Well, I can't say I'm not disappointed," Frank admitted, "but I'm happy for you too. I think this thing between you and Marty has been in the works for a long time."

"You could say that," Wyatt said with a chuckle. "It only took me my whole life to see what was right in front of my nose this whole time."

"Sometimes that's just the way life goes. The important thing is that you've figured out what you want and you're serious about going for it."

"I am," Wyatt said softly, assurance filling him. He was glad his father understood where he was coming from. "Thanks for understanding, Dad."

"You got it, son. Let me know if you change your mind."

"I won't be changing my mind."

"I thought not," Frank chuckled, "but I had to put in one last plug for the shop!"

Wyatt laughed. "Talk to you soon?"

"You got it. Bye, son."

Wyatt ended the call and slipped his phone back into his pocket. He stared at the wall for a long time, contemplating the call he'd just had with his father. The offer to be a partner for a new shop had come out of nowhere, and his initial reaction had been one of excitement. He'd really wanted to say yes to his dad's offer—had he made a mistake? He was passing up a big opportunity...

No, he thought fiercely. *I did the right thing.*

Things with Marty weren't official yet, but he wanted them to be, and he needed to take the risk of passing up this business opportunity if it meant being with her. He knew that he still had a lot to prove when it came to Marty, and this was just one way that he could show her that he truly did want something lasting with her. He had made the right decision, even if it had been a difficult one to make. Marty was worth the sacrifice, plain and simple.

Grabbing the screwdriver again, he crouched beside the dirt bike and was just about to get to work when the bell at the front door jingled. Wyatt set down the screwdriver and headed for the front, pleasantly surprised to see Darla and Rick coming in. He smiled, waving at them and hurrying over to them.

"Darla! Rick! Nice to see you both," he said, reaching out to shake Rick's hand and giving Darla a hug.

"How are things going with your shop? I've heard good things around town," Darla said, smiling up at him.

"Good, good, can't complain."

"Glad to hear it!"

"What brings you in today? Are you looking for a quad?" he asked, looking back and forth between Rick and Darla.

Rick laughed. "Not quite. But, if we're ever in the market for one, you're the first place we'll visit."

"Good to know," Wyatt replied with a chuckle. "What can I do for you?"

"Well," Darla said, leaning forward excitedly,

"Rick and I are hosting a game night and we wanted to invite you and Marty to come."

"A game night," Wyatt said, rubbing his chin. Game nights weren't his usual speed, but it could be fun. "Sounds like a good time! When is it?"

"Tomorrow night, at our place," Rick responded. "You in? Charity and Monica will be coming as well."

Monica Grey was the local librarian, and Charity Turner ran Seastar Espresso. Wyatt didn't know them well, but he knew they were both good friends of Marty's.

"Nice. I haven't seen the two of them in ages," Wyatt said, rocking back and forth on his heels. "Sure, if Marty is in, I'm in."

"Excellent!" Rick said, fist bumping Wyatt. "We're looking forward to it. Bring your A-game."

"You already know I will," Wyatt joked. "Prepare to have your butts kicked."

"At what, Uno?" Rick teased. "That's a game of chance, man."

"To you, maybe," Wyatt shot back. "I happen to be a pro at Uno."

"You can't be a pro at Uno," Darla said, rolling her eyes but laughing nonetheless. "Besides, we'll be playing lots of other games."

"Bring it on," Wyatt said, grinning wickedly. "I happen to be really good at games, any variety."

"We've been warned," Darla said with a laugh. "So, we'll see you tomorrow night?"

Wyatt nodded. "See you then."

Darla and Rick waved at him and then turned to leave. Wyatt watched them go, surprised by how excited he was for the game night. It was much slower than his usual speed for leisure activities, but it meant spending more time with Marty and her family and friends.

It's not so much what you're doing, it's who you're doing it with, he realized with a start, and warmth spread through him.

Who he would be spending the game night with made all the difference, and he couldn't wait to have an excuse to see Marty again.

CHAPTER TWENTY-TWO

Marty shifted the bag of wine and snacks into one arm so that she could open the back door to Darla's kitchen. The bag teetered, nearly falling, and Marty regained her balance just in time. Thankfully, the back door opened a moment later and she saw Charity standing on the other side.

"Marty! Do you need a hand with that bag?" Charity asked, already reaching out to help.

"That would be great," Marty said, puffing a little. "Thanks."

Charity took the bag from her and Marty stepped inside, dropping her purse onto a chair at the kitchen table.

"Phew, I just about dropped it all out there," Marty admitted, smiling at Charity.

"Glad you didn't! You brought all the goodies!" Charity said, poking through the bag and pulling out two bottles of wine. "Where would our game night be without this?"

"A lot less fun," Marty joked.

"Want some help putting the snacks together?"

"I'd love some," Marty said. "I brought fixings for a charcuterie board—crackers, cheese, grapes, prosciutto, you know, things like that."

"Yum! I love a good charcuterie board. This is a step up from the game nights I used to go to in college. Then it was cheap beer and Doritos."

"We're not in college anymore, that's for sure," Marty said with a chuckle.

"Don't remind me," Charity replied, touching her face and rolling her eyes. "You know, I think I spotted a wrinkle when I looked in the mirror the other day?"

"Oh, stop, you look amazing!"

"See? This is why I keep you around. You're a true friend." Charity winked at Marty, which made her laugh.

"Just calling it like I see it," Marty shot back, giving her friend a sassy smile.

Marty began pulling the food out of the bag and setting it out on the counter, then headed over to the sink to wash her hands. Charity was quiet, leaning against the counter and waiting for her turn to wash her hands. As Marty dried her hands off on a clean towel, she studied Charity's face. Now that they weren't talking and joking around, she saw the weary lines that Charity's face had fallen into. Charity still looked beautiful, as she always did, but she seemed to be folding into herself, almost falling off her feet with a bone-deep weariness that worried Marty. She reached out and touched Charity's arm and Charity looked over at her, eyebrows raised.

"Hey, is everything okay?" Marty asked softly.

Charity sighed, reaching for the towel and drying off her hands. She wrinkled the towel up and finally met Marty's eyes. "Not really, but I'm managing."

"What do you mean?"

Charity sighed, rubbing at her forehead. "I'm just tired." She forced a smile. "A game night is just what I need, honestly. I need to get my mind off things and just have some fun for once."

Charity pulled out a colander and unpacked the grapes into it, beginning to rinse them off. Marty watched her for a moment, noticing the tight set of Charity's mouth and the way her eyes drooped with exhaustion.

"Charity?"

"Hmm?"

"Is it your divorce? Is that what's going on?"

Charity set the grapes down and sagged against the counter, giving Marty a tired smile. "I never could hide anything from you, you know."

Marty let that remark pass by, waiting for Charity to answer her question.

"Yes, it's mostly the divorce," she finally admitted, rubbing at her forehead again and looking so weary that Marty impulsively reached out and gave her friend a long hug.

"What's going on with your divorce?" she asked when they broke apart.

"It's just emotionally draining, you know?"

"I can only imagine..."

"Things are mostly settled, but I'll be glad when I don't have to deal with court hearings and lawyers anymore, let's just put it that way. And I want it all to be over so Lucas can get some sense of normalcy back."

Marty nodded sympathetically. "Is there anything I can do?"

Charity gave her a wan smile. "Just being there for me is enough. Thanks for checking on me. I really do appreciate it."

"Anytime. I wish I could do more."

"It'll end at some point," Charity said softly. "I just have to keep hanging in there."

"You're so strong," Marty said, reaching out and squeezing Charity's arm.

Charity gave a laugh, but there was little mirth in it. "I don't feel strong, but thank you."

Charity picked up the grapes again and began destemming them while Marty got out a wooden cutting board to use for the base of the charcuterie board. Marty began unpackaging crackers and arranging them on the board, the two friends working in companionable silence for a while. Charity arranged some grapes on the board and then looked up at Marty with a smile.

"So... things seem to be going well between you and Wyatt," she remarked, giving Marty a searching look and a knowing smile.

Marty bit her lip.

"Oh, no," Charity said. "I know that look... what's wrong?"

Marty sighed, reaching for the prosciutto. "I don't know. I'm trying to open up to Wyatt more, because I honestly feel like he might be the one." She sighed again, pulling a face. "And I know how cliche that sounds, believe me."

"It's not cliche if it's real," Charity said softly. "Go on."

"Well, I really do feel like he might be the one, but I'm... I'm afraid of the risk."

"You still feel like Wyatt is a risk? I thought you said that he'd changed a lot since you were younger."

Marty arranged some prosciutto on the board before responding. "He has," she admitted. "But I'm still scared." She met Charity's eyes and the truth came spilling out. "When I was at his house painting the other day, I accidentally stumbled into a box of old photos from his first marriage."

"Oh, no..."

"Exactly," Marty mumbled. "They just looked so happy together, and I..." she trailed off.

"You started to compare yourself to his first wife?" Charity finished for her.

"Something like that," Marty admitted. "I guess it kind of gave me cold feet. What if I don't compare? What if I bore Wyatt to death with my love of stability and my fear of taking risks?"

Charity reached out and squeezed Marty's arm, taking her turn to be the reassuring one. "I really don't think that's the case."

Marty sighed. "But how can you know that?"

"I guess no one can *know* anything for sure, but I

can tell you what I've observed." Charity paused, collecting her thoughts. "Any time I see the two of you together, it's beyond obvious that Wyatt is falling head over heels for you. It's just in the way that he looks at you, like you're the only person in the room, or maybe even in the world."

Marty paused, searching Charity's eyes. "Does he really look at me that way?"

Charity nodded. "He really does. It's like he forgets that other people are around when you're there."

"But... what about his divorce? He wasn't ready to settle down the first time. What if he's not ready now?"

Charity bit her lip, looking tired again.

"I'm so sorry," Marty hurried to say. "I shouldn't have brought up divorce."

"No, no, it's okay." Charity paused, arranging some cheese on the board before answering. "I know the possibility of things going wrong is scary, but you can't let that stop you. I hope you're not letting my divorce, or Wyatt's, discourage you from opening your heart."

Marty looked down at her hands, not sure how to respond to that.

"If you want my advice..." Charity began, then waited.

Marty looked up and nodded eagerly. "Please."

"Well, I would tell you to open your heart to the possibility of happiness and just take the leap. You have friends and family who are here ready to support you, no matter what happens."

"I'm scared," Marty said in a small voice.

"So be scared," Charity replied kindly. "And do it anyway."

Marty blinked, then nodded. It was so simple, but it made sense. Still, as soon as she opened the floodgate, other fears immediately began to plague her.

"What is it?" Charity asked. "I can see from your face that something else is wrong."

"It's just that... I'm not sure how to proceed with dating Wyatt. I mean, I know he would take me as I am, but I want to meet him halfway. Why should he have to be the only one to make changes?"

Charity nodded thoughtfully, the charcuterie board forgotten.

"I mean," Marty continued. "He's trying to show me that he's putting down roots, that he's reliable and steadier now. So, I want to show him that I can become a bit more adventurous myself." She paused, thinking. "You know, it's not even just for Wyatt. For so long, I've let fear hold me back, and I really think it's time for me to expand my horizons."

Charity reached out and squeezed Marty's hand. "I think that's a great idea!"

"You do?"

"Of course."

Marty smiled. "I'm not really sure how to begin, though."

Charity waved that away. "Not to worry. You've got me!"

Marty laughed. "And just what are you going to do for me, hmm?"

Charity laughed too. "Well, for starters, I'm going to help you concoct a plan to surprise Wyatt with an adventure. We're going to show him an exciting time."

Marty paused, her eyes wide with excitement and some nervousness. "Really? You have ideas?"

Charity nodded eagerly. "You bet."

"Well... okay, then. I would love your help!"

Charity turned back to the board, arranging some roasted almonds on it. "Perfect. We'll put our heads together and come up with something perfect."

"Something perfect for what?" a voice said

behind them.

Marty jumped and whirled around to see Wyatt standing in the doorway, smiling at them.

"Sorry," Charity said teasingly. "Girl talk! No boys allowed."

Wyatt lifted his hands in surrender, backing away and grinning at them. "My bad. I see I've stumbled into a situation where I'm not wanted."

Marty swatted at Charity. "You're always wanted around here," she assured him.

Wyatt looped his arm around her waist, pulling her close and kissing her nose. "Thanks for having my back," he joked. "Charity was trying to kick me out."

"Oohh, these snacks look great," Darla said, coming into the kitchen then. "Thanks, you three!"

"I can't take credit," Wyatt said. "I just got here. It was all Marty and Charity."

"Well then, thanks, you two," Darla amended. "Rick and I have got the games set up in the living room. Do you need help bringing in the snacks?"

"If you could bring the wine and wine glasses in, that would be great," Marty replied.

"Done," Wyatt said, already reaching for them.

"Why, thank you," Darla replied.

All of them trooped into the living room, finding

comfortable spots. Marty sat on the sofa and, to her surprise, Wyatt lowered himself to sit cross-legged on the floor in front of her legs so he could lean against her. She ran her fingers through his sandy hair and smiled, feeling utter satisfaction with the moment.

"Now then," Rick said, leaning forward and rubbing his hands together. "Who's ready to get their butt kicked in Charades?"

CHAPTER TWENTY-THREE

Wyatt was deep in a dream about quad racing when his alarm blared, shattering his dream and pulling him to consciousness. He groaned, rubbing at his eyes, and slapped at the alarm clock on his bedside table with more force than was strictly necessary.

I really need to change my alarm tone, he thought, staring up at the ceiling with bleary eyes. *I'm starting to hate that particular sound. I need something soothing to wake up to, like classical music...*

Making a note to himself to change his alarm clock settings, Wyatt yawned widely and stretched until his limbs shook, then he rolled over and grabbed his phone off his bedside table. He blinked in the bright light of the screen as it turned on, but gradually his eyes adjusted and he smiled when he saw that Marty had texted him.

MARTY: Hey, I had a lot of fun last night! I hope you had a good time too.

Wyatt blinked until his vision focused again and then tapped the message thread so that he could send her a reply. The game night with Darla, Rick, Monica, and Charity had been a lot of fun—even more fun than he had been anticipating. It was much slower than his usual leisure activities, but there was still a competitiveness that was a blast. Plus, of course, spending time with Marty and her loved ones had been wonderful. He and Marty had been quite the team in Charades and she had roundly defeated him in Scattergories and Scrabble, but he hadn't minded. He'd loved seeing Marty's eyes light up with interest and fun as she had played the games and that alone had made the whole evening worth it. He quickly tapped out a reply.

WYATT: I had so much fun! By the way, you looked so beautiful last night.

He hit "send" and then had another thought.

WYATT: The only thing better than us kicking butt at all the games was the kiss we shared after.

He grinned to himself as he set his phone down, tucking his hands behind his head and smiling up at the ceiling. He could picture Marty blushing as she read his text message, her lovely cheeks slowly turning a bright shade of pink. He loved it when she blushed like that, especially when he was the cause. Bantering with her was so much fun—almost as good as kissing her, which he thoroughly enjoyed.

His phone buzzed, alerting him that Marty had responded.

MARTY: Well, thank you. I can't lie, that kiss WAS pretty good...

MARTY: Hey, can you meet me at Seastar Espresso on Tuesday at 8 p.m.?

Wyatt wrinkled his brow as he reread the text. He knew for a fact that the shop was closed that late. Why would she ask him to meet her there so late? He quickly sent her a response.

WYATT: I can do that, but what's up? Why are we meeting there?

Her response came quickly.

MARTY: You'll see. ;)

WYATT: Is that really all I get?

MARTY: Yes, it is, Mr. Impatient. You'll just have to wait until Tuesday to see.

WYATT: Sigh... as you wish...

MARTY: I like the sound of that. ;)

WYATT: Well, there's more where that came from. :)

MARTY: Haha, good! I'll see you on Tuesday then.

Wyatt grinned to himself again as he set his phone down, having thoroughly enjoyed bantering with Marty.

So she has some sort of surprise for me.

Wyatt's grin broadened as he thought about their conversation. Just what did she have up her sleeve? He couldn't wait for Tuesday to find out, and he took it as a great sign for their relationship. It was just more evidence that turning down the offer from his dad to partner in another shop was the right call, and that all of this would be worth it.

I really, really want to be with Marty, he thought, not for the first time. *And... I think I'm falling in love with her.*

The thought was stunning enough to propel him to his feet and he began pacing his room, excitement coursing through him.

"I'm falling in love with Marty Sims," he said

into the quiet room, just to hear it said aloud, and his excitement grew.

His childhood best friend was now becoming the woman he loved, and he couldn't be happier. He was bursting to tell her, but caution warned him that it wasn't time yet, that he needed to take this slowly. He really didn't want to scare her away by jumping the gun—that was the last thing he wanted.

But maybe the time to tell her would come soon. And maybe, if he was lucky, she would tell him she felt the same way too. The thought sent sparks coursing through him and he closed his eyes, imagining Marty's face, blushing slightly, as she told him she loved him back. That moment would mean everything to him. He just needed to be patient and let it play out.

Whistling, he headed into the bathroom and turned on the shower, a spring in his step. Tuesday evening couldn't come fast enough for him.

CHAPTER TWENTY-FOUR

Wyatt checked his watch—7:45 p.m. That meant it was finally time to walk to Seastar Espresso to meet Marty. Their mysterious meetup had been on his mind all day, so much so that he'd had more than one customer have to repeat themselves because he'd been too lost in his own thoughts and daydreams. Whistling, he left his house, locking the door behind him, and sauntered down the sidewalk toward downtown Whale Harbor.

Excitement hummed through his bones as he walked and, with the salty breeze on his face, he felt so alive. Who knew that he could get this kind of rush without being on a quad? It looked like he had been right about love being its own kind of adrenaline, and he liked it. He liked it a lot.

"Hey, Wyatt," one of the townies called to him as he walked past.

He lifted his hand in greeting but didn't stop to chat. He didn't want to be late to meet Marty. Not tonight of all nights.

A few minutes later, Seastar Espresso appeared further up the street. To his surprise, the windows were dark, as though the shop were closed. Hadn't Marty said that it wouldn't be a problem that they were meeting there after hours? He had assumed Charity would keep the shop open for them or something like that but, as he got closer, he saw that he had been wrong about that. He hurried up to the door, where Marty was nowhere in sight, and tugged on it. Locked.

Brow furrowed in confusion, Wyatt checked his watch. 8:00 p.m. on the dot, and Marty was always punctual. He craned his neck looking up and down the street but there was no sign of her. Shrugging, he lowered himself onto the front step, almost crushing a box as he sat down. He picked it up curiously, surprised to see his name written on the top of it in Sharpie. Excited, he opened the box to find a cream cheese Danish—his favorite—and a small, handwritten note.

Enjoy this little treat to start,

But please don't take too long.
Your next clue waits, my heart,
At the place where you get groceries.
(PS sorry the last line didn't rhyme...)

Wyatt burst out laughing as he reread the little note. So Marty was sending him on a scavenger hunt! Very interesting.

Wyatt bit into the Danish, the cheesy, flaky goodness filling his mouth and he sighed with pleasure. Tonight was looking like it was going to be a very fun night.

Brushing crumbs off his waffle-weave long sleeve shirt, he reread the note. So, he needed to go to the place where he got groceries. That could only mean the Harvest Grocery Store. Sure, there was a Walmart a town over where he sometimes shopped, but he was pretty sure that Marty wasn't going to have him leave Whale Harbor. Getting to his feet, he tossed the now-empty box into a nearby trash can and headed down the sidewalk toward the grocery store.

He whistled as he walked, eyes alight, already picturing Marty at the end of the scavenger hunt. The only thing that could make this scavenger hunt better was if she was with him, but he supposed that sort of defeated the purpose.

It only took him a few minutes to walk to Harvest Grocery and soon he was walking through the double glass sliding doors. The store was abuzz with activity as shoppers hurried to get their grocery shopping done so they could get home before dark. Outside, the sun was beginning to set, painting the sky in glorious color. Wyatt looked around himself, not quite sure where to start.

Was he supposed to search every aisle looking for his next clue? That could take all night—or more—if it was just hidden on a scrap of paper.

He pursed his lips, thinking hard. Marty wouldn't have done that to him, he was sure of it. He just needed to be smart about this.

One of the owners, Gus, was walking away from the cash registers toward his office in the back. Wyatt took a chance and hurried over to him.

"Gus! Wait up!"

Gus turned around, breaking into a smile as he saw Wyatt rushing toward him.

"Wyatt! I thought I might see you here tonight."

Wyatt grinned. "Does that mean you have a clue for me?"

"If you're referring to the scavenger hunt Marty set up, then yes, I'm your man."

Wyatt sighed with relief. So his hunch had been correct. "Excellent! Do you have it on you?"

"Matter of fact, it's in my office, along with a couple of treats Marty picked out for you."

"Treats?"

"Yup, come on back and see."

Wyatt followed Gus back to his office. Gus opened the door, apologizing for the mess of papers on his desk, which Wyatt didn't care about in the least. Sitting in the middle of his desk was a bag of flaming hot Cheetos and a bag of ranch flavored sunflower seeds, Wyatt's favorites. How had she known? He guessed she must have been paying more attention to his likes and dislikes all these years than he had realized, and the knowledge made his heart beat harder with adoration for her. She was so thoughtful.

"Here are your snacks," Gus said, handing over the Cheetos and the sunflower seeds, "and here's your next clue."

Wyatt took the paper and read:

Have a treat, but don't you stop,
Your next hint is at your shop.

So Marty wanted him to go to Wyatt's Quads, huh?

He grinned at Gus, thanking him for his help,

and rushed out of the office, weaving his way through the crowds of the grocery store. He only narrowly avoided colliding with an elderly woman whose basket was full of cabbages, but he spun out of the way just in time.

He took a deep breath of fresh air as he left the grocery store, glad to be out of the crush of people so he could hurry toward his shop. This was a moment that he was grateful the downtown area of Whale Harbor wasn't enormous, because he hadn't brought his car and otherwise this would take forever.

A few minutes later, he was slipping into his shop and flipping on the lights. He looked around, realizing this time that he would have to do his own hunting because there was no one to ask for help.

He began at the front desk, searching along the length of it and checking the shelves beneath it. No luck. He stepped out onto the showroom floor, checking all of the quads one by one, but nothing turned up. Then, inspiration struck him. He hurried to the back where he kept his own quad parked.

Bingo.

There, sitting on the seat of his personal quad, was a little scrap of paper.

You've found the next clue, you busy bee,
For your last stop go to Rick's boat

And there I'll be.

(Yes, the rhymes are awful, please don't judge me!)

Once again, Wyatt burst out laughing at Marty's silly note. She really *was* pretty bad at rhyming, but he loved that she had made an effort to make the clues cute. It was just one more sign of her thoughtfulness, and he adored it. He was about to hurry out of the shop when he turned and looked at his quad. He could get to the docks a lot faster if he took his quad...

Decision made, he hopped on and drove out of the back garage door, heading for the harbor, the quad growling with power beneath him. The light outside was fading, but the street lamps had come on and he could still see clearly. He leaned into the speed, relishing the breeze on his face and tousling his hair as he rode. Leave it to Marty to put together the perfect evening for him.

Marty twisted her silver bracelet anxiously around her wrist. She sat on Rick's boat—which he had agreed to lend her—waiting for Wyatt to show up and kept looking at the ever-darkening sky. She hoped he would make it before nightfall. While she waited, she looked over her outfit for the hundredth time, hoping Wyatt would like it. She had picked out a flowy floral jumpsuit and had swept her hair up into a loose bun with curls falling down from it. She knew that it was silly to have done her hair since they were going out on the water, but she had wanted to look extra special for Wyatt that night.

While she waited, her thoughts turned to Wyatt, as they so often did anyway. Her heart warmed as she remembered their date on the dunes and the game night they had just attended together. He was just so much fun to spend time with and he was a dizzying combination of familiar security and heart-racing excitement all at once. Her heart began to beat faster just from the thought of him and she had to laugh at herself a little bit for getting so swept up in him when he wasn't even there yet. The truth was, she had made her decision—she was ready to take a leap of faith and trust with Wyatt. And it felt amazing.

This scavenger hunt idea of Charity's had been wonderful, just the thing she needed to show Wyatt that she was up for adventure. And not just adventure, that she was up for the risk of getting serious about someone—Wyatt Jameson, to be specific. How she hoped that her sweet friend Charity would also have a happy ending in store. She deserved it so much.

Her thoughts were interrupted by the familiar growling sound of a quad roaring toward the dock. She leapt to her feet, coming to the edge of Rick's boat and watching as Wyatt rode up and then parked. Her heart began hammering even harder in her chest, even as she lifted a hand in greeting and tried not to look like her heart was about to beat out of her chest. Wyatt climbed off the quad and raced up the dock to her, climbing onto Rick's boat and pulling her into his arms, swinging her around in a circle before setting her down. She laughed at his exuberance, entirely swept up in the moment.

"Oh, Marty, you are such a gem!" he exclaimed, swinging her around one more time for good measure.

"Put me down, put me down," she gasped between bouts of laughter.

Wyatt set her gently onto the deck and lowered his head to kiss her. She wrapped her arms around his neck, entirely getting lost in the kiss and practically swooning at the feeling of his lips on hers.

"This scavenger hunt was so fun," Wyatt said when the kiss finally ended. His eyes were alight with excitement and she could tell that he really had had a good time, which warmed her heart. "Thank you for putting it all together."

"Well, it's not over yet. Rick has lent us his boat so we can take it out on the water for a spin."

"Are you serious?"

"Yup! He showed me how to work it, but I figured you would be able to help me, too, just in case. No matter what, it should be an adventure, right?"

"Definitely. I've piloted a few boats in my time. Between the two of us, we should be just fine." Wyatt looked into her eyes. "Mar, this is seriously so perfect, thank you."

Marty smiled up at him. "I just wanted to show you that I have an adventurous side too." She paused, a fear coming over her. "It's not too over the top, is it? This is about as risky as I get."

Wyatt wrapped his arms around her waist, pulling her closer. "It's perfect, seriously. I couldn't have asked for a better evening."

Marty felt her heart beat harder as his eyes strayed from hers down to her lips and then back up again. Her eyelids fluttered shut just as Wyatt lowered his lips to hers once again, this time the kiss sweet and deep. They stayed that way for a long time, but when they finally broke apart, Marty's heart was singing.

"Wyatt, I..." she began, and had to take a deep breath. It was time to tell him how she felt. "I really, really like you. Like a lot." She looked up at him, knowing she was blushing but not caring. "Like, a *lot*."

Wyatt gave her that crooked smile she loved so much. "I'm glad to hear it," he whispered, "because I feel exactly the same way about you."

And with that, Marty found herself caught up in a kiss that sent all her thoughts scattering to the wind.

CHAPTER TWENTY-FIVE

The blaring of his alarm woke Wyatt at 5:30 a.m. the following Tuesday. Instead of being angry that his sleep had been interrupted, Wyatt found himself already excited and ready to face the day. The reason? He had invited Marty to come over and help him finish painting the living room before they each headed off to work. Sure, it was insanely early, but getting to see Marty more than made up for any lost sleep.

Yawning so widely he felt like a boa constrictor, Wyatt stumbled out of bed and walked into the bathroom, turning on the shower and waiting for the water to heat up. While he waited, he brushed his teeth, already daydreaming about seeing Marty in the next half hour or so. He found himself chuckling around his mouthful of toothpaste. He was like a giddy schoolboy with a crush—it was ridiculous, and he knew it, but he couldn't seem to wipe the smile off his face.

Humming, he spit out his toothpaste and rinsed his mouth and then hopped into the shower. His humming turned into full-on singing as he stood beneath the hot water, scrubbing his hair and belting out "Surfin' USA" by the Beach Boys. He savored the feeling of the warm water cascading over him, enjoying his morning shower. Was this how everyone felt when they fell in love? Like every experience was brand new and better than ever? He didn't know, but he sure hoped the effects of new love didn't wear off quickly.

Still singing, he turned off the shower and began toweling off, grabbing his phone from the bathroom counter to check the time and realizing that he needed to hurry and get dressed because Marty would be there any minute. True to her strict sense of punctuality, Marty rang the doorbell not five minutes later, just as Wyatt was zipping up his jeans. He hurried to the front door, pulling it open, a smile already playing around his lips, and then groaned.

"Are you kidding me?" he asked.

Marty raised her eyebrows, looking confused. "What?"

Wyatt folded his arms, leaning against the door frame, and shook his head. "It's just not right, Mar. It goes against every law of nature that you can look *this* good at six in the morning."

Marty burst out laughing, warmth rising in her cheeks. "I look normal."

Wyatt shook his head again, reaching out to pull her into the house and dropping a kiss to her forehead. "You look absolutely stunning, and don't even fight me on it."

Marty looked down at her paint-splotched overalls, her eyebrows inching even higher. Her wavy hair was pulled into two braids and she looked, in a word, adorable.

"Um... if you say so," she finally said, still laughing a little.

"I do say so," he declared, wrapping his arms around her and giving her a loud, smacking kiss on the lips, which only made Marty laugh even harder.

She finally pulled away, one hand going to her stomach, which was growling loudly. "You promised me breakfast if I came over before work. Time to pay up, mister."

"So I did," Wyatt acknowledged. "Come on into the kitchen and keep me company while I cook."

Marty trailed him into the kitchen while he pulled some eggs out of the refrigerator and turned the coffee machine on. She took a seat at the table, watching him contentedly while he cracked eggs into a warming skillet and began scrambling up some eggs.

"Anything I can do to help?" she asked after a moment.

"Could you throw some bread into the toaster?" he asked. "It's in the cupboard by the sink."

"Sure thing."

They worked in companionable silence for a moment, Wyatt stirring the eggs in the skillet and the sound of the coffee pot percolating filling the kitchen. When the toast popped, Marty foraged around for a butter knife and began buttering the hot toast, then she set the table with two plates, some utensils, and two mugs. Wyatt divided the scrambled eggs onto their two plates and then reached for the coffee pot.

"Be it ever so humble," he murmured, pouring her a mug of hot coffee. "Breakfast is served. Sorry it isn't fancier."

"It's perfect," Marty declared around a mouthful

of scrambled egg. "Do you have any creamer for the coffee?"

"That I do," he said, rummaging in the fridge and coming back with the creamer. "Is vanilla flavored okay?"

"Oh, yes," she replied, pouring some into her coffee and taking a long, slow sip. "Mmm... I finally feel like a functioning human again."

"Don't talk to me before I've had my coffee, and all that?"

"Exactly. You get me."

"Oh!" Wyatt said, jumping to his feet. "I have something for you!"

He hurried down the hall to his bedroom, where he'd been hiding the bouquet of flowers he'd bought for her, and brought them into the kitchen. When he returned, Marty laid down her fork, looking stunned.

"Those are for me?"

"Of course," he said, pressing a kiss to her forehead. "There's a card in there too."

Marty's eyes were already filling with tears as she pulled the card out of the bouquet. "Wyatt, they're so beautiful. Thank you."

"I'm glad you like them," he murmured, watching her happily.

Marty blinked back her tears but her eyes were

still shiny with teardrops. "Can you read the card for me? The tears are making my vision all blurry."

Wyatt chuckled, taking the card from her. "Of course I can." He cleared his throat and read the card, feeling a little self-conscious. "To the one I care for more than I can say—thank you for saving me and my home from mundanity—you've brought so much life into the space and I couldn't be more grateful."

Marty pressed a hand to her heart, looking touched. "Oh, Wyatt..."

Wyatt could feel himself blushing. "It's nothing."

She reached over and squeezed his hand. "It means everything to me. Thank you so much. This is beyond thoughtful," she said, wiping at a stray tear and giving him a watery smile. "And, it definitely makes getting up at five in the morning worth it."

"I'm glad," he whispered, reaching over and pressing a gentle kiss to her lips. He lingered there for a moment and then sat back. "Ready to get to work?"

Marty scooped up the last bite of her scrambled eggs and nodded. "I was born ready."

"I like your attitude, Ms. Sims."

"I like *you*, Mr. Jameson."

Wyatt laughed aloud, reaching out and kissing her again. "I could get used to hearing that."

They got up from the kitchen table and walked into the living room, picking up their painting supplies. Wyatt poured fresh paint into the paint tray while Marty prepared the roller brushes.

"This is going to look so good when it's finished," she said, rolling some paint onto her brush and getting to work on the wall.

"Kudos to you for picking out the color."

"Hey, it's kind of my job," she said with a grin.

"And you're very good at it," he assured her, getting to work beside her.

"You know," Marty said after a minute. "I really like being with you in the morning. What made you think of doing this? Aside from us both having really busy weeks this week and this being one of the only times we could make this happen."

"Well, I have to keep up with you after your scavenger hunt surprise the other evening. I have to keep things spicy or you'll get bored with me."

"I don't think I could ever get bored with you," Marty said seriously, focusing on the painting, then she paused and looked at him. "You know, before you I never would have done something like this, even though this is really not that big of a deal."

"What do you mean?"

Marty searched his eyes. "I just... I was so stuck

in my routine, you know? I never really thought about disrupting it, even in small ways, but you came into my life and gently taught me how to be more open to new things. You've brought both a spark and safety into my life," she finished softly.

Wyatt's heart warmed at her simple words and he felt a lump forming in his throat. He blinked back tears and smiled down at her, placing a finger beneath her chin gently and lifting it so that she was looking into his eyes.

"Thank you," he said softly.

Marty smiled up at him. "If you keep this up, I'll be a whole different person," she teased.

"You may be more open to new things, but you're still wonderfully calm and steady," he said. "And I'm glad. I love you just the way you are. I don't think I need to worry about you getting too crazy."

Marty quirked an eyebrow at him, her expression turning mischievous. "Are you sure about that?"

Before Wyatt could respond she took her roller brush and rolled paint across his nose. He gasped in surprise and then roared with laughter.

"You really shouldn't have done that," he growled, grabbing her around the waist while Marty squealed.

She twisted away from him, trying to run away,

but he had already scooped up some paint from the paint tray and thrown it at her already paint splattered overalls. Marty gasped and then splattered him with paint too. Wyatt charged at her and grabbed her again, knocking them both off balance and they tumbled to the floor, Marty landing on top of him. Their laughter died away as they looked into each other's eyes and then, a heartbeat later, Wyatt's lips were on hers, his hands in her hair, and the only thing on his mind was kissing her for the foreseeable future.

He wasn't sure how much time had passed when they finally broke apart, both breathing a little quicker than usual. Marty's eyes were dazed and wide.

"Whoa," he murmured, and she nodded in agreement. "We should get into painting fights more often."

Marty got to her feet, helping him up. "If we do that, we'll never get your living room painted," she warned him. "Less kissing, more painting."

Wyatt nodded with fake soberness. "Yes, ma'am," he said, saluting her..

Marty laughed, swatting at him. "I meant it. Paint, you."

Wyatt lifted his hands in surrender and then

picked up his roller brush, obediently painting the unfinished wall. When Marty was painting beside him, though, he couldn't help but steal another kiss. And then another.

CHAPTER TWENTY-SIX

"What color are you going to get?" Darla asked, poring over the selection of nail polishes at the spa. "There are so many, I have no idea how I'll ever decide!"

"Hmm..." Marty responded, tapping her finger against her chin and studying the selection as well. "I'm always drawn to the blue tones, myself."

"Blue does look amazing on you," Darla agreed, picking up a crimson red and holding it against her hand to see how the color would look against her skin tone, then setting it back down.

"Thanks. What about that dusty rose? That color always looks nice on you."

Darla picked up the nail polish Marty had been

pointing out and held it up against her hand. "I think we have a winner," she declared happily.

"Yay!"

"And have you picked one?"

"Yup. I'm going with this pale blue. You know me, I like what I like and I don't stray too far outside those lines."

Darla shot her sister a look. "Maybe so, but you're getting better and better about trying new things. Dating Wyatt suits you."

Marty smiled at her sister, looking more confident, carefree, and happy than Darla had seen her in a long time. "Thanks, sis. Should we take our colors over to our nail techs?"

"After you."

The two sisters sat down side by side and the nail techs began working on their nails, prepping them for painting. They were in the middle of a glorious spa day, and Darla couldn't be happier that Marty had come along with her. They had already gotten blowouts—after deep tissue massages and facials first, of course. The last stop after getting their manicures would be to get their makeup done. Darla had been surprised that Marty had been all about spa day, but she was glad Marty had suggested it in the first place. They hadn't been pampered like this in a long time. In fact, Darla couldn't remember the last time she'd had a good spa day, but this one had been fantastic so far and she was feeling like a whole new woman.

"Your nails look so healthy," Marty commented, looking over at Darla's hands. "Mine are always so fragile. How do you do it?"

"I've started taking a collagen supplement, and it's really helped."

"Ooh, I'll have to look into that!"

The two sisters continued chatting about trivial things as the nail techs painted their nails, enjoying each other's company and the chance to sit back and be taken care of for a change. After another twenty or so minutes, their nails were all done and the two were stopping for a cucumber water before going to the makeup artist.

"What kind of look are you going to go for?" Marty asked as she took a sip of her water.

"Something sophisticated and understated—I don't want to look like a completely different person."

"Oh, same. I don't want Wyatt getting ideas about the level of goddess I should be looking like every day. Who has time for that?"

Darla laughed. "I know what you mean. My

makeup routine is pretty much just mascara and a little bit of lip gloss."

"Because you have perfect skin," Marty commented, rolling her eyes. "That's why that's all you need."

"Hey, you have perfect skin too. We share the same genes," Darla reminded her with a laugh.

"Yeah, but yours is practically glowing."

"I'm telling you, it's the collagen," Darla said, finishing up her cucumber water. "Ready for our makeup appointments?"

"Lead the way."

Darla walked into the makeup studio and took a seat the stylist pointed out for her, swiveling to face the mirror. The stylist asked her what kind of look she was going for, and Darla pulled up some pictures on her phone, showing her some examples of chic but understated eyeshadow and a light contour. Marty sat beside her talking to her stylist as well. Within a few minutes, the stylists had set to work, applying and blending their desired makeup looks.

"Whoa," Darla said, blinking at her reflection, somewhat dumbfounded as the stylist finished up. "This looks amazing. Thank you!"

"You're very welcome," the stylist responded. "The colors you picked out suit you perfectly."

"Thanks," Darla responded, getting out of the seat.

Marty stood as well, looking absolutely breathtaking. As they walked out of the spa together, Darla felt like a whole new woman—and she liked it. They were just approaching Marty's car when Darla's cell phone rang. She fished it out of her purse and saw Gabrielle Watson's name on the screen. She slid the green button to answer the call.

"Hey, Gabrielle, what's up?"

"Darla? I was wondering if I could ask you for a favor..."

"Fire away."

Mrs. Watson took in a deep breath. "I know you're probably busy, but if you're not, I could really use your help at the school. I have to duck out for an emergency and I need someone to cover my class. Is there any chance you're free?"

Darla smiled. "I'd be happy to help. Do you need me to come over now?"

"If you could, that would be amazing."

"I'll see if Marty can drop me off. I'll be there soon."

"Oh, you're an angel! Thank you so much!"

"Don't mention it, really."

Darla said her goodbyes and then hung up,

turning to Marty, who was already pulling her keys out of her purse.

"Do you need a ride somewhere?" Marty asked. "I caught part of the phone call."

"Mrs. Watson needs me to cover her class, it's some sort of emergency. Could you drop me by the school?"

"I'd be happy to. Not a problem."

"Thanks so much!" Darla said, climbing into the passenger seat.

Marty started up the car, laughing a little as the radio blared the Spice Girls at them from their drive to the spa.

"Whoa, I'm not the same person I was a few hours ago," she declared, turning the station to something softer.

"Right? I hate it when that happens," Darla agreed. "Okay, I've got to figure out what I'm going to do with the kids if Mrs. Watson doesn't leave a lesson plan."

"Well, it's almost the end of the school day," Marty pointed out after looking at the clock in the car. "You could pick out a book from her library and read it aloud to them. I always loved it when the teachers did that in school."

"Better than showing them a movie, which was

my other option," Darla said, chuckling. "I like it. Great idea!"

A few minutes later, Marty parked the car in front of the school. "I'll come in with you," she offered. "Just in case you need help with crowd control."

"Are you sure?"

"Yeah, it's no biggie," Marty assured her.

"Thanks! You're full of helpful surprises today," Darla teased.

The two walked into the school, making their way down the long hallway full of children's artwork and posters about school events. Darla smiled as she saw some of the art she had helped with in her art classes. It always filled her with pride to see her students' work. Mrs. Watson's room was just up ahead. She pulled open the door, expecting to see Mrs. Watson waiting for her, but instead, to her surprise, Rick stood at the front of the room.

She felt her forehead wrinkle in confusion. What was Rick doing there? Then, a moment later, seeing that she had arrived, Rick signaled to the students and they held up homemade posters that read, "Darla, will you marry me?" as he lowered himself to one knee. Darla felt herself beginning to tremble, her eyes swimming with tears as her jaw dropped.

"Rick?" she whispered.

"Darla," he said, taking her hand and smiling up at her, his eyes full of love. "I never expected you to come back into my life, but when you came back to Whale Harbor, you changed my whole world. Now, I can't imagine a life without you in it. I want to keep building our life together, to have a family with you." He paused, swallowing, and squeezed her hand gently. "Will you, Darla Sims, make me the happiest man on earth and become my wife?"

Darla covered her mouth with one trembling hand, entirely unable to speak around the lump in her throat. Her heart was dancing and electricity hummed through her. All she could do was nod, over and over, and finally whisper, "Yes, a thousand times, yes!"

Rick sprang to his feet, pulling her into his arms and kissed her in front of all the kids, who squealed, which made Rick laugh against her lips. He let her go, sliding a gorgeous emerald cut diamond ring onto her finger. It fit perfectly and she held up her hand to the light, admiring its sparkle.

"It's perfect," she whispered, nuzzling into Rick's

chest and wrapping her arms around him. "Oh, Rick, I'm so happy!"

"Me too," Rick replied, lowering his head to kiss her again, this time not caring that the kids squealed and cheered.

When they broke apart, Darla looked around to see Marty and Mrs. Watson watching and smiling, clapping along with the kids. She realized now that the entire day had been set up—Rick must have asked Marty to take her to the spa, and Mrs. Watson had lured her to the school.

"You planned all of this?" she asked Rick, her heart swelling with love. She didn't think it was possible to love him more than she already did, but somehow today had taken things to the next level.

Rick nodded. "With lots of help from these kiddos and your sister."

"I can't believe you went to so much effort for me."

"I would do it all again and more. You're worth it."

Darla cupped his face in her hands, laughing and crying at the same time. This man standing before her, her Rick Maroney, was the man for her. She was certain of it, down to her very toes. Everything in her life had led her up to this moment and she thought she might burst with the joy of it all.

"I can't wait to become a family with you," she whispered.

Before Rick could reply, the kids came up, no longer able to sit still in their seats, and began hugging them. Still laughing and crying, Darla hugged them back, thanking them for helping Rick with his proposal. Mrs. Watson approached her next.

"Congratulations, sweet girl," she said, reaching out to hug Darla. "I couldn't be happier for you."

"Thank you so much. And thanks for helping Rick plan this."

"My part was very small, but I was happy to be a part of things."

Marty came up to her then, throwing her arms around her sister and hugging her tightly. "Oh, Darla," Marty whispered into her hair. "I'm so happy for you!"

"Thank you! It's still so surreal," Darla replied, looking into her sister's honey brown eyes. "I hope one day you feel this same happiness."

"I'm sure I will," Marty said, smiling softly.

Darla didn't mention his name, but she wouldn't be surprised if that person who brought her sister the same kind of happiness she was experiencing would be none other than Wyatt Jameson. Ever since the two had started dating, Marty had seemed happier and more confident. She was still herself, but she was more too. Darla loved to see it, and she hoped things continued to progress well for her sister.

"We'll have to tell Mom," Marty was saying, already pulling out her phone. "Here, let me snap a picture of you and Rick to send to her!"

Rick and Darla posed, Darla's hand, engagement ring flashing, resting on his chest. Marty snapped the picture then checked it.

"Perfect! Do you want me to send this to Mom?"

"Actually, not yet," Darla said, threading her fingers through Rick's. "I think the two of us would like to tell her in person."

Rick nodded and Marty smiled.

"She's going to be over the moon about this!"

CHAPTER TWENTY-SEVEN

Marty held up first one outfit in the mirror, then another. Her room was scattered with clothes already as she mercilessly hunted through her closet to find the perfect outfit to wear for the October Showdown. Essentially the whole town would be there—it was a huge event, with booths and food and games, as well as, of course, the big race. Marty hadn't been in a few years, and when she had gone, she never really watched the races. Not this year. This year, Wyatt's race was her main focus and she would be there at the front of the crowd, watching him compete.

How can I have this many clothes and still have nothing to wear? she thought desperately, pulling out another outfit and looking in the mirror.

It was a black silk jumpsuit, very chic and understated, but very elegant. Right for a fancy dinner occasion, but not for the laid back atmosphere of the October Showdown. She groaned, hanging it back up and folded her arms, glaring at the clothes in her closet.

"I'm going to have to wear jeans, aren't I?" she grumbled, going over to her dresser and pulling out her favorite pair of boyfriend cut jeans.

It wasn't that she hated jeans, it was just that she liked dressing up more than wearing them, but this wasn't the place for her jumpsuits or palazzo pants or her other stylish clothes. She pulled the jeans on, pleased to see that they still looked perfect on her, and then hunted through her tops for something casual yet chic. She finally settled on a black see-through top that she would wear over a black camisole. It looked excellent with the jeans and it was definitely a step up from a t-shirt, which was what most other folks would be wearing.

Satisfied with her outfit, she pulled on a chunky silver bracelet that Darla had given her—simple yet punchy—then moved on to the bathroom to do her makeup. Like Darla, she didn't typically wear very much makeup, but she took extra time curling her eyelashes before applying her mascara and she also decided to put on a subtle nude eyeshadow that shimmered in the right lighting. It was the little details, she had found, that made a difference. After swiping on some clear lip gloss, she pronounced herself ready to go—and just in time too.

Just as she was sliding her cell phone into her back pocket, she saw Wyatt's Jeep pulling up her driveway. She opened the door and waved to him, then grabbed her keys and hurried outside, locking the door behind her.

"Hey, cutie," he greeted her, jumping out of the Jeep to open the passenger door for her. "Looking good."

"Oh, this old thing?" she teased, as though she hadn't just spent the last hour searching for the right outfit.

Wyatt closed the door after her and she buckled her seat belt while he walked around the front of the Jeep and then climbed back into his seat. Thankfully, this wasn't an open Jeep, or it would ruin her hair, teasing her curls beyond all reason—or any hope of detangling. Wyatt turned the key in the ignition and the car roared to life.

"Want some music?" he asked, his hand hovering above the radio knob.

"How about some classic rock?" she asked.

Wyatt paused and turned to stare at her, his jaw dropping open. "Are you serious? I didn't think you liked classic rock."

Marty scrunched up her nose, smiling at him. "Maybe you don't know everything about me."

"Be serious, do you actually like classic rock?"

Marty couldn't help but laugh. "In the right conditions, yes. I think it's the perfect thing to get you revved up and ready for the Showdown."

"You've got that right," Wyatt agreed as he tapped "Highway to Hell" by AC/DC on his phone and the opening notes blared out of the speaker.

Marty winced, turning the volume down. "I may like some classic rock, but not that loud!"

"My bad, I was jamming out while I was coming to pick you up," Wyatt apologized.

Marty twisted in her seat to look at him as he drove out of the driveway. "How do you have any hearing left if you listen to music that loudly?"

Wyatt flashed her a boyish grin, cupping a hand around his ear. "What?"

"I said, how do you—" She broke off, realizing the joke. "Oh my gosh, you!"

"I promise I only jam out with the music that loud on rare occasions," Wyatt said, steering the car out of her neighborhood. "Like today. I have to get hyped for the Showdown." He bobbed his head to the music. "Of course, if you pick the right songs, I guess it doesn't *have* to be blasting to still be motivating."

"That's the spirit."

"What are you looking forward to most today? The funnel cakes? The food trucks?"

Marty swatted at his arm. "Watching you compete, obviously."

"Well, that's a given," he teased back. "Seriously, aside from the actual Showdown, what are you looking forward to the most?"

"Hmm..." Marty pondered the question for a moment. "I'm going to have to go with browsing through the booths. Sometimes I stumble across some really good pottery or art pieces that I buy to sell in my shop."

"I hadn't thought about that. Do you source a lot of your wares locally?"

"When I can. It's important for me as a small business to support other small businesses. Plus, when I find custom pieces, it means that people can trust that my shop isn't just a mainstream retailer. It adds to the charm and authenticity of the place." Marty broke off, realizing that she was rambling.

"Sorry, sometimes I just get excited when I talk about my shop."

Wyatt reached out and grabbed her hand, squeezing it. "Don't apologize for being excited. I love hearing you talk about what you're passionate about."

"Thank you. That means a lot." Marty looked out the window at the beautiful scenery passing by. They were on a curvy road that sometimes afforded views of the ocean, and she loved catching the little glimpses of the wide blue expanse.

"Besides, I'm sure that I do the same thing when I talk about dirt bikes and quads."

"Only sometimes," she teased.

"Hey!"

"Just kidding, just kidding."

Wyatt pulled the car into the designated parking for the dunes and killed the engine. He suddenly got very quiet, and Marty knew he must be thinking about the upcoming race. She squeezed his hand, waiting until he looked at her.

"You're going to be amazing," she said softly. "I just know it."

"I hope so. I'm excited but..."

"But still a little nervous," she finished for him.

"Yeah. Which sounds so stupid."

"It doesn't sound stupid," she defended. "This race is really important to you. I'd be surprised if you *weren't* nervous, at least a little."

"Just don't let my competitors know," he joked back. "I would lose all my street cred."

"We can't have that," she teased back. "My lips are sealed."

"This is why I keep you around, cutie."

Wyatt opened his door and hurried around the Jeep to open the door for Marty. When she was standing in the parking lot, he wrapped his arms around her, heedless of the crowds of people walking over to the dunes.

"Can I have a good luck kiss?" he asked, looking deeply into her eyes.

"You don't even have to ask."

Marty raised up on her tiptoes and, throwing her arms around his neck, she kissed him deeply. And then once more for good measure.

"Good luck," she whispered.

Wyatt looked a little dazed when he opened his eyes. "I wish I'd had that good luck charm before all of my other races. But I guess it matters the most because this is my last race."

Marty blinked, cocking her head to the side. "What do you mean?"

Wyatt smiled softly. "This Showdown is going to be my last official competition. I'll still ride quads and run my shop, but I don't need this kind of thrill like I used to. Riding for fun is enough for me."

"Wow," Marty finally said. "I never thought I'd live to see the day that you voluntarily stopped racing."

Wyatt shrugged, then winked at her. "I guess you don't know everything about me either." He took a step back. "Okay, I need to go prep for the race. I'll watch for you in the crowd."

"I'll be at the front, cheering my heart out for you," Marty promised.

Wyatt beamed at her. "I wouldn't have it any other way. Okay, see you after the Showdown!"

Marty waved and watched as he sauntered away. She couldn't believe he was giving up racing, but a part of her was relieved. It was just one more indication that Wyatt really had changed for the better. She loved that they were both working toward a common middle ground. She was opening herself up to adventure and risk, and Wyatt was becoming more steady and dependable.

Marty headed toward the main area of hubbub, where booths were set up and food trucks lined any open spaces. She knew that Seastar Espresso was going to have a booth, and that Darla and Rick were bringing some of their dune-inspired paintings to their own booth to try to make some sales. As Marty wove her way through the throngs, she realized that she felt less out of place than she had at the last race.

Maybe that feeling of being an outsider, she thought. *Maybe that was all just in my head the whole time.*

The feeling gave her comfort and she realized she *did* belong. She belonged because she wanted to be there for the man she was falling for. It was as simple as that, but the knowledge buoyed her up and made her feel more confident and open to the whole experience.

Marty shifted past a cute little family waiting in line for cotton candy and, as she did so, she spotted Darla and Rick's booth. She hurried over to them, pulling Darla into a hug, then greeted Rick.

"You guys, your paintings look amazing!" she said, taking in their booth. "These are awesome!"

"Thanks," Darla said. She leaned forward conspiratorially. "We've already sold two!"

"That's wonderful! I'm not surprised, honestly."

Darla nodded, then looked at Marty closely. "And how are you doing? Are you nervous about Wyatt's race?"

"I was before," Marty admitted. "And I guess I still am, a little, but mostly I'm excited for him. This is going to be his last race, and I hope it goes really well."

Rick checked his watch. "The race starts in a few minutes. Should we go grab a spot to watch it?"

"Of course!" Marty said. "I want to be right at the front."

As they walked together to the area roped off for watchers to stand, Marty could feel the excitement in the air. It was that palpable. She took in a deep breath of salty air, loving the contrast of the blue ocean with the sandy dunes. The sky arched overhead a perfect blue, not a cloud in sight. It was the perfect day for the Showdown.

As they took their places, Marty searched for Wyatt among the riders. When she found him, she waved and he waved back. She could tell he was grinning like a schoolboy beneath his helmet. The excitement of the crowd was even more intense now that the race was about to begin, and Marty could feel it humming in her veins.

"Riders, take your places," the announcer said over the loudspeaker. "On your mark... get set... go!"

The racers took off, their quads flying forward. Wyatt leapt to the front, revving ahead in a spray of sand. Marty cheered, whooping and clapping as she watched him crest the first dune, catching major air. Her heart leapt at the sight but she reminded herself that he would be okay. She relaxed into the fun of the event, watching Wyatt narrowly outmaneuver other racers and keep his place in the lead.

He soared up another dune and then, at the top, she watched in horror as another quad swerved into him, sending his quad flipping over and over down the dune as though in slow motion. Marty screamed, surging forward along with the medics, heedless of their cries for her to get back behind the ropes. She clawed her way forward, racing across the sandy dunes, just behind the medics. As she ran, all she could think over and over was, *Please let him be okay, please let him be okay, please let him be okay.*

CHAPTER TWENTY-EIGHT

The first thing Wyatt became aware of was the smell —antiseptic. He swallowed, feeling the dryness in his throat and struggled to open his eyes, but his eyelids were like lead weights. He could hear a soft steady beeping somewhere nearby, something machinelike. He furrowed his brow, concentrating. What was going on? Why couldn't he open his eyes?

With a herculean force of will, he managed to pry open first one eyelid, then the other. At first he could see nothing, it was all a blur, but then gradually his vision cleared and he found himself staring at a pale green wall with a generic painting of wildflowers. He blinked, confused. Where in the world was he? He turned his head ever so slightly and took in the sight of hospital equipment—so that was the source of the beeping. Why was he in the hospital though?

He tried to shake his head, but stopped quickly when a spear of pain shot through him. He winced, closing his eyes and exhaling slowly. Ever so slowly, his memories came back to him. He had been racing at the October Showdown when something had gone wrong. He remembered cresting the top of one of the highest dunes, and then feeling a hard thud against his quad, sending his quad flipping through the air, the dunes flashing wildly across his vision. That was the last thing he remembered before all went black.

"Wyatt? Are you awake?" a soft voice asked.

Wyatt opened his eyes again and turned to the side to see Marty sitting in a chair by his hospital bed. Her eyes were tight with anxiety, her brow furrowed. He tried to smile at her, but he was afraid it probably looked more like a grimace. He opened his mouth to speak, but his throat was too dry.

"Here, do you want some water?" she asked.

Wyatt gave a slight nod and Marty hurried to his bedside table to pour him a plastic cup of water from the pitcher resting there. She put a straw in it and then held it up to his lips. He took a long sip, sighing with relief.

"That's better," he croaked when he was

finished, leaning back against his pillow with another sigh. "Hey, don't look so worried," he murmured, seeing that Marty's look of extreme anxiety had not softened the least bit.

"It's hard not to," Marty whispered. "I mean, I watched you fly through the air. I watched the medics load you into an ambulance."

"I'm so sorry. I didn't mean to worry you."

"You don't need to apologize. I'm just glad you're all right."

Wyatt paused, feeling extremely tired. "What... what happened?"

"You were hit by another racer and it made your quad flip," Marty explained, her voice tight. She reached out and rested her hand on his, which was when he became aware that his wrist was covered in a cast. "You have a concussion and you broke your wrist. Oh, Wyatt... it could have been so much worse."

"And that's the important thing to remember," he said softly. "It could have been so much worse, but it wasn't. All in all, I think I got off pretty easy, all things considered."

A tear slipped out of Marty's eye and trickled down her cheek, making Wyatt's heart ache.

"Oh, love," he murmured. "I'm so sorry I scared you."

"It's okay," she whispered, her voice strangled.

"No, it's not. But, you don't need to worry anymore, because that was my last race. I meant what I said. Come here, sweetheart," he said, patting the bed beside him.

"Oh, I don't want to hurt you."

"It won't hurt me," he promised. "Come here."

Gingerly, she climbed onto the bed, curling up beside him. He put his arm around her, pulling her close as she wept against his chest. He ached for her, knowing that outcomes like this were exactly the reason she was afraid of taking risks. He could only imagine how frightened she had been when she'd seen him fall off his quad, could only imagine her panic as the medics had rushed to him.

"But what about racing?" she finally asked. "You love it so much."

"I'll still ride my quad, just recreationally," he said. "I'll still have fun, but it will be lower stakes."

Marty bit her lip, wiping at her eyes. "I just... I don't want to hold you back. I feel like you're having to give up your love of adventure for me, and I hate it."

Wyatt shook his head, then stopped when the

pain lanced through it again. "No, it's not like that," he promised her. "I'm looking to have a new kind of adventure. One that isn't so much about adrenaline or death-defying acts. Something else." He paused, running his fingers through her dark brown hair. "I have something else to tell you."

Marty shifted, looking up at him. "What is it?"

Wyatt took a deep breath. "My dad offered me a partnership in a new quad shop one of his employees is opening up—"

"That's amazing!"

"—and I turned it down," he finished.

Marty blinked, clearly shocked. "What? Why? That doesn't make any sense. You love your shop, and you'd be invaluable for the new one. Plus it means expanding your business."

"Sure, it does mean all of that," he acknowledged. "But here's the thing, it would take me away from Whale Harbor all the time. All the time," he repeated, to make sure she understood his point. "I don't want to be away from you all the time, and taking on that partnership would mean not seeing you as much. So, just like deciding I'm not going to race quads anymore, I decided to say no to this so that I could say yes to another thing—being with you."

"Oh, Wyatt, are you sure? This is a big opportunity to pass up."

"You matter more to me than any 'opportunity', can't you see that? And don't tell me you're not worth it, because you very much are. Marty, you're everything to me."

Marty's eyes filled with tears again and she snuggled closer to his chest, wrapping her free arm across him.

"Thank you," she whispered. "You have no idea what it means to me to have you say that."

"As for giving up adventure for you," he continued. "I'm not. I'm just saying yes to having *new* adventures with you, which will be way better than anything I've done in the past. And these adventures don't have to be crazy or super risky or anything like that. They can be whatever you like. As long as I'm with you, it will be an adventure."

"Do you really mean that?" Marty searched his gray eyes, begging him to be honest with her.

"With my whole heart," he whispered, brushing a kiss against her forehead. "We don't have to go kayaking or mountain climbing or zip lining. As long as I'm spending time with you, I'll be on the best adventure of my life. Falling in love with you has already been that for me."

Marty's breath caught and she stared up at him. "In love... ?"

Wyatt nodded. "Marty, I love you. I didn't tell you before because I didn't want to scare you away, but I need you to know now. I love you so much it hurts."

Marty's lip trembled and she covered her mouth with one hand, new tears springing into her eyes. "And I love you," she finally whispered. "I can't believe I just said that aloud."

"I'm glad you did." He chuckled. "Or this whole situation would be really awkward!"

Wyatt was pleased when Marty laughed. He loved the sound of her laugh—it was one of his favorite sounds in the whole world.

"Wow," she said, resting against his chest once more. "I can't believe fate brought us back together. Who would've thought? Younger me would die knowing I'm with Wyatt Jameson, and that he loves me back!"

"Younger Wyatt Jameson was an idiot. I can't believe it took me so long to see what was right in front of me all along."

"Hey, don't talk badly about your younger self. I've been in love with him for so many years."

"But you love the current Wyatt Jameson, too, right?"

"More than ever," Marty promised. "More than ever. Falling in love with you this time has been the greatest adventure of my life too."

"Here's to a lifetime of adventures together," Wyatt whispered, cradling her face in his good hand.

He lowered his lips to hers, kissing her long and slow, feeling Marty's hand tangling in his hair. He laughed against her lips as the heart rate monitor beside him began beeping faster. Marty laughed too, but it was quickly drowned out as he pressed another kiss to her soft lips.

How he loved this woman in his arms, and this was only the beginning of their journey together. He couldn't wait to see what their future would bring.

CHAPTER TWENTY-NINE

"I can't believe people already have their Christmas decorations up," Wyatt commented as he drove through downtown Whale Harbor.

Marty tossed him an amused glance. "What do you mean? Thanksgiving was a couple of days ago—if anything, it's the people who don't have decorations up who are behind."

"Let me guess, you already have your tree decorated at home."

"Guilty as charged, and not a bit ashamed either," Marty said, sticking out her tongue at him.

Wyatt pulled into the parking lot for the beach and killed the engine. "You sure about walking on the beach? It's a bit chilly out."

"Come on, where's your sense of adventure?"

Marty teased. "You're going to let a little cold stop you from seeing the best sunset in Whale Harbor?"

"Challenge accepted," Wyatt said promptly. "I should never have doubted you."

"No, you shouldn't have," Marty agreed cheerfully.

Wyatt walked around the Jeep to open her door for her, helping her out of the car. Wyatt had been right—it *was* chilly out, but Marty didn't mind. Wyatt had already slung his arm around her shoulders, tucking her close to his side, and she nuzzled into the heat his body provided, grateful for her warm jacket as well. They began walking down the beach, their shoes sinking into the cold sand and the sound of the gentle ebb and flow of the tide greeting them.

"Somehow it never gets old," Marty commented.

"What never gets old?"

"The beach. These views. It's always as majestic as if I'm seeing it for the first time," she said, taking in a deep breath of the salty air.

A seagull cawed over head, wheeling in the darkening sky. The sun, a huge orange orb, sank toward the horizon. Marty rubbed at her arms and snuggled closer to Wyatt as they walked.

"I dare you to dip your toes in the water," Wyatt

said after a moment, his eyes gleaming with a challenge.

Marty blinked. "Are you crazy? The water is freezing!"

"That's fine. I guess you're just too chicken..."

Marty glared at him even as she laughed. "Nobody calls me a chicken and gets away with it," she warned, already bending down to untie her shoes.

She stripped off her socks, the cold sand squishing up between her toes.

"Come on, I'm not doing it alone," she said. "Shoes off, mister."

"I guess it's only fair to do it myself if I challenged you," Wyatt agreed with a boyish grin. "Last one in the water is a rotten loser!"

Marty squealed as Wyatt tugged her back and then sprinted for the water, chasing after him. She slowed as she reached the water, dipping a hesitant toe into its icy depths.

"Oh, come on, you can't do it like that!" Wyatt called. "You have to just run into it!"

Marty took a deep breath and then, squealing, raced into the water. The iciness of it took her breath away and she gasped for air.

"Wyatt, you're a monster!" she yelled, teeth chattering.

"Who are you calling a monster, hmm?" He raced toward her, accidentally splashing her with more water.

Marty yelped, scooping up some water and splashing it on him. It was Wyatt's turn to gasp and he snatched her around the waist, pulling her out of the water and spinning her around. He set her down on the sandy beach just as a wave came in and sloshed them both to their knees, almost knocking them over again.

"Can I cry uncle?" Marty gasped, laughing and shaking with the cold. "I give up, I give up!"

"Yeah, it's freaking cold in there," Wyatt agreed, grabbing her hand and racing with her out of the water. "Whose idea was that?"

"Only yours, you brilliant, brilliant man," Marty said, her voice dripping with sarcasm that she softened with a quick kiss on the cheek.

Wyatt wrapped his arms around her, pulling her close against him and looked down into her eyes. "Just trying to keep up with you, my little daredevil."

Marty laughed, rolling her eyes at his ridiculousness. The past month had been incredible. She and Wyatt had been all but inseparable, spending every spare minute that they could together. Now that they were both all in, it was like they couldn't get enough of each other. Marty was having a blast stepping out of her comfort zone in little ways and trying new things as she and Wyatt explored Whale Harbor together.

Even though she'd grown up there, it was like she was experiencing everything for the first time, especially as Wyatt encouraged her to try new things. Marty was, in a word, in heaven. She'd had no idea her life could feel like this, and she wouldn't trade her new life with Wyatt for anything.

"Ugh, I'm never going to get all of this sand out of my toes," Marty commented, plopping down onto the sand to find her shoes and socks.

"Work with it, not against it," Wyatt advised. "Use it to help dry your feet off. No one likes soggy socks."

"Too true," Marty agreed, rubbing her feet into the sand. "I still stand by what I said—it's going to take forever to get all the sand out of my socks and shoes."

"Hazards of visiting a beach. Worth it."

"You know what, it really is a small price to pay," Marty agreed, leaning against his shoulder.

Wyatt wrapped his arm around her, resting his

head against hers as they watched the sun sink below the horizon, the sky above streaked in majestic yellows, oranges, and pinks. They were quiet for a time, simply enjoying the sunset and each other's company. Finally, though, Marty's shivering got the best of her.

"You're shaking, love," Wyatt said, rubbing her arm.

"I think it's from getting into the water when it was already cold out," Marty replied, her teeth chattering.

"Come on, let's get you to my house and I'll make you some hot cocoa. I think I have some sweatpants you can change into. They'll be super baggy on you, but they'll be warm."

"That all sounds divine," Marty said, scrambling to her feet and then reaching down to help Wyatt up. "Let's do it!"

"Slow down there, cowboy," Wyatt said with a laugh. "We still have to put our shoes and socks back on."

"Oh, right." Marty laughed, looking down at her bare, sandy feet.

She bent over, pulling her socks on and wincing at all the sand still stuck to her feet, then pulled on her shoes and tied them up. When she finished,

Wyatt was already waiting for her. He threaded her fingers through his and kissed her hand, then tugged her back toward the parking lot.

"What, you're not going to challenge me to race to the car?" Marty teased.

"Nah, I'm just enjoying the moment with you," Wyatt said, warming Marty's heart full to bursting with love.

She paused, pulling him close and raising up on her tiptoes to kiss him. At first, she'd been shy to initiate kisses, but the more time they spent together, the easier it was getting for her to put herself out there and show him just how much she loved him.

Back at the Jeep, Wyatt opened the passenger door for her, ever the gentleman, and helped her climb into the Jeep. Soon they were back on the road and heading to Wyatt's house, the radio blasting Christmas songs while they sang along, challenging each other to see who could sing the loudest. Marty laughed as she realized she was flirting with Wyatt like a schoolgirl, but she didn't care. She was having too much fun.

Back at his house, Wyatt unlocked the door and let them both inside. Marty, who had thawed out a bit in the car, was looking forward to stripping off her wet jeans and pulling on Wyatt's warm sweatpants.

True to his word, he emerged from the bedroom with them a moment later.

"And here are some fuzzy socks for you too," he said, handing over a fresh pair of bright red fuzzy socks.

Marty raised an eyebrow. "I didn't know you owned fuzzy socks..."

"Hey, just because I'm a manly man doesn't mean I don't love creature comforts like everyone else," he joked.

Marty laughed and thanked him, changing into the sweatpants and socks and leaving her wet things in a laundry basket so she could take them home later to wash them. She wandered into the kitchen where Wyatt was preparing them the hot cocoa he'd promised her back at the beach. She inhaled the heady aroma of chocolate and came up behind Wyatt, wrapping her arms around his waist and resting her cheek against his back.

"The hot chocolate should be ready any minute," Wyatt promised her.

"Okay. I'm in no rush. Thanks for the sweatpants and the socks."

"No problem, love."

Marty let go of Wyatt and wandered around the living room, looking at all the new furniture and decor, thinking of how nicely it had all come together. Wyatt's home had been a bare bachelor pad before she'd stepped in, but now it was really cozy and homey. A moment later, Wyatt joined her, two mugs of hot chocolate in tow.

"Here you go," he said, handing her one. "We earned it! And we'll have to keep earning hot chocolate throughout the winter by skiing and sledding and such."

"One never has to 'earn' chocolate," Marty said with some asperity. "It's simply a God-given right."

"My bad, my bad," Wyatt said with a laugh.

"That painting by Darla looks really good hanging up," Marty commented, taking a sip of her cocoa. "It really ties the whole room together."

"I agree," Wyatt said, studying the artwork. "You know, everything you did in this house looks amazing." He hesitated, looking at her searchingly. "That being said, there's still something missing..."

Marty furrowed her brow, looking around. To her way of thinking, they'd thought through every detail and it had come together beautifully. "What do you mean?"

Wyatt swallowed, looking nervous. "Well, I think it's missing a woman's touch... and a certain woman. You." Wyatt paused, taking a deep breath as

Marty's heart began to race. "Marty... I know we've only been together a little over a month, but I'm ready to take the next step with you. I want you to move in with me."

Marty blinked, staring at him, and she knew her jaw had dropped open. "Are you serious?"

Wyatt looked embarrassed. "I knew it was too soon, I'm sorry, I—"

Marty cut him off with a gentle finger to his lips, a smile blooming on her face as she thought her heart might burst with love. "No, it's perfect. I just wanted to make sure you meant it, because I would love to move in with you!"

Wyatt whooped, pulling her into his arms carefully so as not to slosh their hot chocolates, and kissed her deeply. Marty returned his kiss, pouring all of her love for him into it. She couldn't believe that this man she'd had a crush on since she was a young girl was her perfect match. She couldn't believe that they had reconnected and found love when they least expected it, but it was happening and it was perfect.

They complemented each other in the best ways. He brought out her adventurous side, and she helped him to be more steady and dependable. They had found a middle ground where each of them was their best selves, and Marty loved what they had.

When the kiss finally ended, Marty took a deep breath and looked around, seeing his house with new eyes. It wasn't just his house, it was *their* house. When she had been decorating it with him, she'd had no idea that she was also decorating her future home, but it was perfect.

"I'm so glad you said yes," Wyatt said softly, kissing her forehead. "I can't wait for you to live here with me."

"Me too," Marty whispered, raising up on her tiptoes and pressing a sweet kiss to his lips. "I hope you realize I'm not the only one moving in with you."

Wyatt pulled back, his brow wrinkling in confusion. "What do you mean?"

"I'm a package deal. Don't forget about Peaches, Trouble, Bertram, and Macy."

Wyatt laughed aloud then nuzzled her nose. "As if I would forget them, I know they're the ones who really call the shots!"

Marty chuckled too, kissing the tip of his nose. "And don't you forget it!"

ALSO BY FIONA BAKER

The Marigold Island Series

The Beachside Inn

Beachside Beginnings

Beachside Promises

Beachside Secrets

Beachside Memories

Beachside Weddings

Beachside Holidays

Beachside Treasures

The Sea Breeze Cove Series

The House by the Shore

A Season of Second Chances

A Secret in the Tides

The Promise of Forever

A Haven in the Cove

The Blessing of Tomorrow

A Memory of Moonlight

The Snowy Pine Ridge Series

The Christmas Lodge

Sweet Christmas Wish

Second Chance Christmas

Christmas at the Guest House

The Saltwater Sunsets Series

Whale Harbor Dreams

Whale Harbor Sisters

Whale Harbor Reunions

Whale Harbor Horizons

Whale Harbor Vows

Whale Harbor Blooms

Whale Harbor Adventures

Whale Harbor Blessings

For a full list of my books and series, visit my website at www.fionabakerauthor.com!

ABOUT THE AUTHOR

Fiona writes sweet, feel-good contemporary women's fiction and family sagas with a bit of romance.

She hopes her characters will start to feel like old friends as you follow them on their journeys of love, family, friendship, and new beginnings. Her heartwarming storylines and charming small-town beach settings are a particular favorite of readers.

When she's not writing, she loves eating good meals with friends, trying out new recipes, and finding the perfect glass of wine to pair them with. She lives on the East Coast with her husband and their two trouble-making dogs.

Follow her on her website, Facebook, or Bookbub.

Sign up to receive her newsletter, where you'll get free books, exclusive bonus content, and info on her new releases and sales!

Made in United States
North Haven, CT
05 December 2024

61700527R00174